Suntastic Fun

THE C☀MPLETE SERIES

ARIELLA ZOELLE

Cover Design by Cate of Cate Ashwood Designs

Editing by Pam of Undivided Editing

Proofreading by Sandra of One Love Editing

Layout by Ariella of Sarayashi Publishing

ISBN: 978-1-954202-11-5

Dedication

To all of our friends who make summer fun so exciting.

it might be hot

SUNTASTIC FUN ☀ BOOK ONE

ARIELLA ZOELLE

it might be hot

SUNTASTIC FUN ☀ BOOK ONE

ARIELLA ZOELLE

Dedication

May we all have summers as hot as Lachlan and Alessandro's.

Chapter One

ALESSANDRO

WHEN I ARRIVED at Lachlan's beach house, I found him relaxing on a rainbow unicorn float in his pool. I had given it to him as a joke when he moved in a few years ago. It never failed to amuse me he had an unironic delight for it that was in stark contrast to his macho masculinity.

As I drew near, I took a moment to drink in the sight of his chiseled body on full display. I had spent years fantasizing about worshipping every inch of him until he came while moaning my name. I'd love to feel his long arms and legs wrapped around me as I pleasured him. I dreamed of the day I could run my fingers through his sandy-blond hair as I held on while he fucked me stupid. Sadly, his endless parade of girlfriends meant I'd never be lucky enough to spend a night in his bed, let alone the rest of my life.

It was hard not to chuckle at his petulant pouting

that drew my attention to his full lips I'd die for the chance to kiss. I had to tease him about it at least a little. "How can you sulk while riding a unicorn?"

"Easily." His lower lip jutted out further to tempt me even more. "Hey, Alessandro."

Stripping off my T-shirt, I sat on the side of the pool and let my legs dangle in the water while I got acclimated to the temperature. "What's ruining your day?"

Our friend Callahan came over with a smirk. He was fair-skinned, with auburn hair that was even more red in the sunlight. "I bet I only need one guess." He kicked off his flip-flops, took off his blue T-shirt, and did a cannonball into the pool, causing Lachlan to yelp when he got splashed.

Baxley had a broad build, and an infamous playboy smile. He also was a notorious flirt and prankster, so he followed Callahan's example by stripping and then cannonballing into the pool to once again douse Lachlan with the water spray.

Callahan high-fived him for the solid follow-through. "That was a ten out of ten, my friend."

"Thanks. Is Lachlan still moping about his ex-girlfriend?"

The man in question scowled. "I'm allowed to!"

"Come on, you didn't even like her that much." Callahan stretched out to float on his back. "Then again, you were together, what? A whole month? That's practically a record for you." It was a fair point when Lachlan was famous for going through girl-friends as fast as some people changed their underwear.

"He liked what she could do for him, but that's about it." I tried not to be jealous of that fact.

He made a noise of protest. "That's not true!"

"Oh, really? Name me something you miss about her that doesn't involve sex." Baxley waited a few heartbeats to give him a fair chance to answer. "See? You can't think of anything not involving what she could do for you."

Lachlan kicked water in Baxley's direction. "What's so wrong with liking how good she was at sucking my dick? Why do I need more than that from a relationship?"

I gave him a break by sliding into the pool instead of splashing him. "It would be a lot less of a headache for you if you let me blow you rather than hoping you'll find a woman who only mildly annoys you." I had offered countless times during our six years of friendship, praying he'd take me up on it. "You at least like me."

He ignored my joking attempt at a pass. "Fine, I'll admit that I miss her talented mouth more than her. Are you satisfied you made me sound like an asshole?"

"Yes," Baxley said with a smirk. It earned him a face full of water when Lachlan splashed him with his foot.

Callahan always looked on the bright side. "Hey,

at least you're being honest about it. She was cute, but she would make any guy want her to suck his dick to stop her from talking. I get it, man. I've been there. We *all* remember Cindy." The reminder made us groan and wince at his awful ex-girlfriend.

"Both of you either need to develop better taste in women or learn how to enjoy being with men," Baxley said, making us all laugh.

"Knowing our luck, their taste in male partners would be just as bad." I could only imagine what kind of hell it would be to see Lachlan bring a cute twink around that was lucky enough to warm his bed. It hadn't happened yet, and I burned with jealousy. I dunked myself to cool off, then ran my fingers through my black hair when I resurfaced.

Lachlan sounded offended. "You think I couldn't land a hot guy?"

"Oh, you could have any man you wanted." Baxley's comment made my envy spark like a live wire. "But if you plan to date the male equivalent of your normal girlfriends, do us all a favor by never switching teams."

Callahan burst into laughter, but I didn't have it in my heart to join in. Instead, I took one last shot. I swam over to Lachlan and ran my hand up his shin and over his knee to rest where his white trunks started. My touch made him shiver despite the warm summer day. "You'd be much better off taking me up on my offer."

"For once in your life, please make a good decision, Lachlan," Baxley teased him. "Let Alessandro show you why you shouldn't spend another moment wishing what's-her-name comes back."

To my surprise, Lachlan seemed to be considering my proposition. I could see myself reflected in his mirror-finished sunglasses as he looked at me. "What's in it for you?"

Making all of my dreams come true. However, there wasn't a chance in hell I was about to admit that out loud. Instead, I chose a more playful retort. "A guaranteed good time for both of us."

"Yeah, but you don't *actually* want to suck my dick…do you?"

"Holy shit, he's thinking about it!" Callahan exclaimed through laughter.

"Clearly, we've underestimated how desperate his dick is to find a willing hole." Baxley snorted, earning him another kick of water in his direction.

Unable to resist, I slid my hand up the inside of his swimming trunks to refocus Lachlan's attention on me. He startled as his thigh tensed under my touch. I gave him my best attempt at a seductive look. "All you have to do is say, 'Please,' and I'll show you pleasures you've never imagined."

"Yeah, right." He scoffed, but I heard the uncertainty underlying his tone. "You're just joking like you always do."

"No, he's definitely serious," Callahan disagreed

with a laugh. "You should take him up on it after all these years. Maybe you'll learn something about yourself."

Since Callahan was the only other straight one amongst us, Lachlan asked his opinion. "Would *you* let Alessandro suck your dick?"

It surprised me he didn't need to think about his answer. "Mouths don't have gender, so sure, why not?"

Lachlan's jaw dropped in shock. "Seriously?"

"What's the big deal? He doesn't have to be in love with me to suck my dick. It'd just be a friend helping a friend. I'd probably even jerk him off afterward as a thank-you."

Baxley swam up behind Callahan and embraced him. "If you're open to other offers, Alessandro isn't the only one here who's interested in cocks."

"I'm almost horny enough to say fuck it, let's do a circle jerk, so don't push it, Bax," Callahan joked as he swam out of his friend's grasp. "I know I've been single for too long when you're somewhat tempting."

Baxley's blue eyes lit up with delight. He had been interested in Callahan from the first moment I introduced them two years ago, but our straight friend seemed oblivious to that fact.

Returning my attention to Lachlan, I stroked his thigh, sending a shudder through him. "So, what do you say?"

When he took too long to answer, Baxley swam

under the unicorn float and flipped it and Lachlan into the pool. We all laughed when he popped up with a splutter.

Pushing his sunglasses up to rest on his head, he wiped the water from his face. "You're such an asshole!"

"Stop pouting like a baby, and let's have some fun!" Baxley poked him in the ribs for good measure.

Lachlan responded by jumping on him and dunking him. It was a weird thing to be jealous of. But finally stirred out of his foul mood, the fun Lachlan I adored came out to play.

Our roughhousing turned into a spontaneous game of water tag. When I was it, I pounced on Lachlan from behind, hugging him like a determined koala. The feeling of our wet skin sliding against each other was heavenly. "Tag, you're it!"

"Are you going to let go of me so I can return the favor?" he asked with laughter in his voice.

I sagged all of my weight against him. "Maybe I want to stay right where I am."

"You hugged the wrong side!" Baxley called out, making us laugh.

It startled me when Lachlan turned in my hold to face me. I was unprepared to suddenly be plastered against his sculpted physique that would put a statue of a Greek god to shame. If I didn't let go soon, his abs wouldn't be the only thing that was rock-hard.

"Is this better?" he asked, his rumbling baritone voice turning me into a puddle.

Risking potential embarrassment, I pressed closer against him as I tightened my legs around his waist. "That depends on what you want to do with me." My heart almost jumped out of my chest when he cupped my ass to hitch me higher. "That's a promising start."

To my great disappointment, he moved his hands to the waistband of my trunks. Clearing his throat, he had the decency to look sheepish. "Sorry, force of habit."

Being bold, I laced my fingers through his hair like I had always dreamed about doing. "I wasn't complaining."

Ever the helpful one, Callahan catcalled us. "Kiss him!"

Having gotten rid of his sunglasses to play, I could see deep into Lachlan's blue eyes. There was a hint of fire there that I wanted to spark into a full blaze. I held my breath as I waited for him to make some kind of move.

In true guy fashion, he responded by dunking me. I laughed when I popped back up to the surface, but it disappointed me he hadn't taken a chance on kissing me.

Maybe someday…

LACHLAN HAD a quirk about loving his pool but hating the chlorine. Why he hadn't switched to a salt-water pool was beyond me. As soon as we finished playing outside, he went to take a shower, leaving me, Callahan, and Baxley alone to chat in the living room.

"You know, for half a second, I really thought Lachlan was going to kiss you." Callahan heaved a disappointed sigh. "Is it weird I was kind of rooting for it to happen?"

Baxley took a swig of his drink. "You weren't the only one." He knew about my feelings after we had gotten a little too drunk once and a confession poured out of me. Like a true friend, he had guarded my secret. But sometimes he couldn't resist teasing me about it. "Right, Alessandro?"

"Hey, a guy can dream." I shrugged as I played with my water bottle.

Callahan surprised me yet again. "Not gonna lie, but even I was a bit tempted by Bax's offer."

One of Baxley's blond eyebrows quirked upward. "What stopped you from agreeing?"

"It's just a running joke between us. Clearly, I've been single too long if I almost took you seriously."

My phone vibrated with an alert on the table. I picked it up to check it.

Lachlan: *Can you come upstairs?*

Alessandro: *Did you fall in to your toilet and need help getting out?*

Lachlan: *Very funny. Get your ass up here now.*

As I typed out a joke response, he beat me to the punch.

Lachlan: *I won't ask again.*

He couldn't really be asking me to blow him, right? I was obviously reading too much into his simple sentence. But I also wasn't about to risk my chance. I announced to my friends, "I'll be back."

"Please tell me you're going upstairs to suck Lachlan's dick." Baxley gave me a wicked grin.

"I'll be pissed if he's only asking me to come up because he's out of toilet paper." My quip caused both of them to laugh. "If I'm gone a while, have a beer in celebration, and don't interrupt our fun."

With those words, I went to find out if my best friend was ready to make all my wishes come true.

Chapter Two

LACHLAN

I HAD OFFICIALLY LOST my goddamn mind. My dick was harder than a diamond, and I was seriously considering letting my gay best friend blow me to make it better. It was just a running joke between us, not a genuine offer. I'd be a fool to take his playful jest at face value.

But alone in my shower, my unruly mind refused to stop thinking about Alessandro's mouth teasing me into a frenzy. I kept imagining what it would be like to kiss him or see his full lips wrapped around my cock. They were outrageous thoughts for a straight man to have, but Callahan's words from earlier kept coming back to me: *Mouths don't have gender, so sure, why not? What's the big deal? He doesn't have to be in love with me to suck my dick.*

It was a persuasive argument, especially when my erection throbbed with an almost painful need to get off. The idea of a man going down on me didn't dissuade my arousal, which meant something. Worst-case scenario, I could always fantasize about the Alessandra female version of Alessandro while he took care of me, right? He was certainly pretty enough to be a woman. Thinking about him dressed up as a sexy woman in lingerie only made me ache more.

When Alessandro knocked on my bathroom door, my prick twitched in anticipation of what might happen next. I kept my back to him to hide my situation until I had sussed out his stance on the matter a little more.

"You summoned me?"

I took a deep breath as I questioned my sanity. But my dick wouldn't suck itself, so I plowed ahead. "How serious were you when we were joking around earlier?"

Although my back was to him, I heard the grin in his voice. "About giving you the best blow job of your life?"

His words made me ache with a desperate need to come. "Yeah."

"Is that it?"

It was a question I hadn't expected. Glancing over my shoulder, I couldn't make out his features through the fogged glass. "Are you offering more?"

"That depends."

I had to know the answer. "On what?"

"What do you want?"

All the blood rushing south made it too hard to think. That meant what little filter I possessed disappeared. "I miss kissing, too."

"Are you inviting me into your shower to make out with you before I blow your dick *and* your mind with my talent? Because that's what I'm hearing."

I reached behind me to push open the glass door in invitation. "Are you interested or not?"

"Oh, I'm interested." The sound of his clothes hitting the floor caused my pulse to spike. "I'm *very* interested." He didn't hesitate as he joined me. When he stood in front of me, to my surprise, he was already hard. More shocking was that wasn't a turn-off. If anything, it was totally doing it for me.

It's just a friend helping a friend, right? That was how I rationalized it to my brain. But the reasoning became unimportant when Alessandro pressed his body against mine and ran his hands up my chest to my shoulders. By the time he entangled his fingers in my hair, my willpower shattered. I leaned down and brushed my lips against his, half expecting him to push me away. But he tugged me closer and opened for me, bursting the floodgates within me.

Backing him against the wall, I pinned him in place as I dominated him with an aggressive kiss full of my pent-up need. He teased me with his tongue, inviting me to claim his mouth for mine. I drank him down like a man dying of thirst, desperate for more.

His whimpers echoed in the shower, driving me wild. When his hand wrapped around my length to stroke me, it ripped a feral growl from me as I thrust into his tight grip.

I burned with a blinding need for more as I lost myself in the perfection of his soft lips yielding to me. His tongue tantalized me with a preview of what I could expect later, driving me mad with lust. There was no sense of strangeness about kissing my male best friend for the first time. It felt like the most natural thing in the world.

Since I had always been an ass man, I couldn't resist reaching down to grope his. It filled me with wildly inappropriate thoughts about rubbing my hard-on between his cheeks and engaging in anal sex. The latter was one of my favorite pleasures my girlfriends rarely indulged. The more I imagined it, the hotter I burned. I fantasized about having him on all fours as I took him from behind, caressing his ass as I plowed him hard. That definitely wasn't a thought a straight man should have about his gay best friend, but fuck if it didn't arouse me even more.

My last remaining brain cell reminded me of what Alessandro had told me earlier in the pool: *All you have to do is say, 'Please,' and I'll show you pleasures you've never imagined.*

"Please, Alessandro." Pride be damned, I begged him with the desperation I felt. "*Please*, I need you."

My plea earned me a demanding kiss as he

rewarded me for doing as he had asked. He then started kissing down my neck and chest, lowering himself as he got closer to my erection. The sight of him on his knees caused my desire to rocket out of control.

He put on a show of teasing the tip with his tongue before sliding me into his mouth. I groaned as he toyed with me, feeling like I'd explode if I didn't get some relief. But my disappointment turned to ecstasy as he stepped up his efforts. He held the base of my cock as he took me deeper with every bob of his head. I shouted when he progressed to letting me glide into his throat as he worked me with a skill that put Charlotte to shame.

I ran my fingers through his hair as he alternated between deep-throating me and teasing the tip while stroking my length. As he picked up speed, I couldn't stop myself from thrusting into the wet warmth of his mouth. Instead of gagging, he stared up at me with a playful gleam in his eyes as he moaned around me. The vibrations pushed me to my limits.

My assumption that I would have to fantasize about Alessandro being Alessandra was mistaken. That it was my male best friend giving me toe-curling pleasure was more exciting than I had ever expected. After all the years of teasing and sexual tension between us, it felt *so* good to finally get relief. It made me regret how long I had written off his playful offers as a joke, because his mouth was fucking *magical*. He worshipped me as if he was born without a gag reflex. I couldn't get enough of him or the experience.

It sent me racing to my peak faster than I wanted. "Fuck, I'm getting close," I groaned, praying like hell he wouldn't stop and finish me by hand. When he redoubled his efforts, I came hard enough to almost see stars. He drank my release down and licked me clean before wiping the corner of his mouth with his thumb. I didn't know why that was so hot, but it was fucking doing it for me. Between his skill and the heat of the shower, I staggered back to sit on the black wooden bench built into the wall.

My breathing was ragged as I tried to recover. "Holy shit, you *really* weren't kidding about that being the best blow job of my life."

He straddled my lap with an arrogant laugh. "That'll teach you to not believe me in the future."

My arms circled around his slender waist as I held him on instinct. His erection pressed against my abs, which surprisingly didn't disgust me. If anything, it was sexy as fuck that giving me oral sex turned him on that much. A lot of the women I had been with had done it as an obligation, but he had sucked my dick like it was the greatest joy life offered.

Once again, Callahan's words rang through my mind: *It'd just be a friend helping a friend. I'd probably even jerk him off afterward as a thank-you.*

After an orgasm that good, it was the least I could

do to repay Alessandro. I reached out with hesitant fingers as I trailed them along his length. "Can I?"

"Do you really want to?"

I wrapped my hand around his erection and worked it. "Yeah, I do." It was a little strange at first to jerk off a dick that wasn't attached to me, but the weirdness of it faded fast. His erotic whimpers as his hips jerked in response to my touch drove me wild in a way I didn't expect. Nor did I anticipate what it would stir to life inside me as he started kissing up my neck while rocking against me with needy noises. As he reached my ear to tug on it with his teeth, I was already half-hard.

Without thinking, I used my other hand to tilt his head to allow me to steal another kiss. Tasting the evidence of my enjoyment on his tongue was the fucking *best*. It got even better when I started stroking both of our erections together. The dual sensation as we made out sent me higher than I ever thought was possible when being with a man. I never would have imagined that Alessandro's breathy moans and whimpers of need would drive me wild. But I wanted more as he submitted to me, feeling drunk with lust and power.

"Lachlan!" That was all the warning I got before Alessandro came all over my stomach.

The last thing I expected was for that to trigger my second orgasm, but the pleasure I derived from making him come pushed me over the edge. I moaned as I shot my load, my cum mixing with his on my abs. Why did the sight of that light my fire into a roaring blaze?

Cupping my face in his hands, Alessandro kissed me hard with a sense of desperation, almost as if he feared it would be our last one. The notion squeezed my heart in a vise. Concern for my friend and the incredible experience made me blurt out, "Please tell me we can do this again!"

He leaned back, allowing me to see the guarded hope in his dark eyes. "Are you serious, or are you only saying that to make me feel better?"

"I'm absolutely serious." After what had happened between us, there was no way I'd be satisfied stopping there. "We *need* to do this again."

Relief washed over him, making it easier for me to breathe. "Tell me when and where."

"How about tonight after Callahan and Baxley leave? Does that work for you?"

His smile was radiant. "Yeah, I think we can have some *real* fun once they're gone."

I wasn't sure what he was promising me, but I wanted whatever he was offering. If what we had done was any indication, I was in for a damn good time.

"HOW DO you want to handle things downstairs?" Alessandro asked as we redressed after our incredible shower.

Maybe it was the satisfaction dulling my mind, but his words didn't connect for me. It also might have been because I was trying to sneak one last peek at his ass before he covered it with his shorts. "Huh?"

He couldn't hold back his grin. "What should we tell Callahan and Baxley? They think I came up here to suck your dick."

"But you *did* come up here to do that." I tried not to remember how good it felt as I finished putting on my clothes.

Alessandro laughed hard. "Yeah, but do you want them to know that?"

"They would assume that even if it wasn't true." It was an unfortunate consequence of all of us being gutter-dwellers about sex.

"Are you okay with that?"

I started to make a cavalier retort, but I stopped myself. If I wanted another chance at experiencing the incredible joys Alessandro's mouth offered and maybe more, I needed to give him a genuine answer and not laugh it off. I held his gaze as I told him, "I'm not ashamed of what we just did."

It was cute watching him fight back a pleased smile. "That's good to know."

Closing the distance between us, I didn't resist my strange urge to reach out and caress the outline of his jaw. "Nothing that amazing can be embarrassing." Something in me urged me to kiss him again, so I did. In a calmer state of mind, I could appreciate how soft his lips were as they parted for me, inviting me to delve deeper for a taste. Even without passionate need fueling my desires, it felt so damn good that I never wanted to stop. "Especially because it would be a lie to say that I don't want more."

His flirty smile stirred me up inside in unexpected ways. "If you keep kissing me, you'll definitely get more. We'll also be in danger of not making it downstairs."

Since I was still tapped out after two back-to-back orgasms, I needed a little more time to recover. "I'll save it for later. Let's get the heckling part over with first."

He laughed as he led the way out of my bedroom, his shorts hugging his ass. How had I never noticed how perfect it was?

Because you were scared you might like it, the voice in the back of my mind answered.

That may have been true in the past, but after such an intense experience together in the shower, it definitely wasn't now. I couldn't wait to have another chance to enjoy Alessandro.

Chapter Three

ALESSANDRO

I COULD FEEL Lachlan's gaze fixated on my ass as we walked down the stairs. It made me put a little extra flounce in my step to show off for him. Blowing him in the shower had been a dream, but I intended to do more with him now that I had piqued his curiosity. I wasn't about to lose my chance of getting to be with him. Even if it was only for one night, I wanted him to be mine.

As soon as we entered the living room, our friends started catcalling. Baxley teased Lachlan, "How much do you regret waiting so long to take Alessandro up on his offer?"

Before he could answer, Callahan hit him with a follow-up question. "Was it worth temporarily switching teams?"

"Are you ready to apply for a permanent transfer?" Baxley added.

Lachlan sat down on a couch, completely unbothered by the questions. "A lot, definitely, and maybe."

I covered my mouth with my hand to hide my shock over his answer. Surely, a single blow job wouldn't be enough to make him seriously consider giving up women, right? I did my best to school my expression into a neutral one as I sat next to him on the couch.

Callahan's grin turned wicked. "Damn, Alessandro. You must have some serious talent to cause a womanizer like him to consider the possibility of being with a man."

Baxley dropped his arm over his friend's shoulder. "He's not the only one, you know. I'm *very* skilled at making persuasive oral arguments if you're interested."

"You didn't take advantage of us being gone by experimenting together?" I tsked in mock disapproval. "I'm disappointed in you both."

"I figured you wouldn't want to walk in mid-blow job," Baxley said with a shrug.

Lachlan snorted in disbelief. "Oh, is that the only reason you didn't jump at the chance to play with Callahan?"

When he didn't answer, I couldn't resist getting payback. "You could have at least made out while you waited. Ease him into it, you know?"

"I'm not sure if I'm ready to learn about that part

of myself yet," Callahan said with a laugh, taking the jests in stride. "I mean, what if I love it? Then what do I do? Bend over and assume the position?"

"You're welcome to try." Baxley gave him a heated look that made his cheeks flush. "Or you could nicely ask for more. I'd never tell you no."

Callahan laughed nervously. "That's a little above and beyond the limits of normal friendship."

"It'd just be taking things to the next level." Baxley reached over and caressed the back of Callahan's neck, sending a visible shiver through him. "We would be even closer friends after that, don't you think?"

Lachlan once again surprised me. "I can confirm that's definitely true. Feel free to use one of the guest rooms upstairs to find out for yourself."

"I'd rather eat lunch," Callahan said. He was obviously uneasy, but I had my suspicions that it had more to do with how tempted he was by being intimate with Baxley. "How does pizza sound to everyone?"

In true Baxley fashion, he leaned over and murmured in Callahan's ear, "Pizza's fine, but I'll save room to make you dessert later."

We all laughed when Callahan squeaked in surprise at the offer. Baxley played it off as a joke, but I knew how badly he wanted his best friend. Luckily, it seemed he was making some progress on his goal.

LACHLAN and I had his place to ourselves after Callahan and Baxley left for the night after dinner. My heart hammered as I waited for him to make his move.

"Do you think they'll go through with it?" Lachlan asked, locking the front door.

"There aren't many people who could turn down Baxley when he's serious about pursuing them. Combined with Callahan's natural curiosity and horniness, I bet they hook up tonight."

"Speaking of which." Lachlan wrapped an arm around my waist, pulling me flush against him. His erection pressed insistently against me, causing my heart rate to spike. "I'm up for some more experimentation if you are."

I swallowed hard, offering a silent prayer asking the cosmic universe to make all my wishes come true tonight. "What are you in the mood for?"

His hand migrated down to cop a feel. "I haven't stopped thinking about this all night."

"And what are you hoping to do?" *Please say fuck me!*

I held on to him for support when he leaned in and started trailing kisses up my neck to my ear. "I keep imagining what it would be like to rub my cock between your tempting ass cheeks."

"Is that all?"

"No, I keep getting turned on by picturing taking you on all fours." That made two of us since that was one of my favorite fantasies I had enjoyed playing out in my mental movie theatre for years. "Being with someone who enjoys anal sex is such a rare treat for me."

I tugged on his shirt to get him to make eye contact with me. "Then you better take me upstairs and bury yourself balls-deep in me, because I won't be satisfied until you come inside me."

My words seemed to break the last of his restraints. He crushed his mouth against mine as he devoured me with lust. I clung to him with a whimper as I let him sweep me away with his passion. It took a monumental effort to stop and go up to his room, where we tore off our clothes before getting in bed.

I made myself comfortable on my stomach to give him unfettered access. He got behind me on his knees, then ran his hands down my back before caressing temptation.

"Your ass is so fucking perfect," he groaned as he continued fondling it. "It's a crime it took this many years for me to appreciate it."

"Aren't you glad you have the chance to make up for it now?"

"That's not all I want to do." Lachlan shifted into a position to allow him to rub his cock between my ass cheeks. He surprised me by keeping it at a slow frot, savoring the experience. "Why have we never done this before?"

"You tell me. I've been making passes at you as long as we've known each other. You're the only one who prevented this from happening." I cursed myself when he stopped what he was doing and moved away. "Sorry, that came out wrong. I—"

He interrupted me as he got off the bed to walk over to his nightstand. "Don't apologize when you're right."

I looked up at him to judge his expression. Other than a furrowed brow of concern, I couldn't tell what he was thinking. "Then why do I feel like you're mad at me for it?"

"I'm not mad at you." He pulled open the top drawer to grab a bottle of lube, then held up a condom. "You said you wanted to feel me come inside you. Does that mean this is optional?"

"It sure does." I grinned when he chucked it back in and shut the drawer.

"Today keeps getting better and better." He positioned himself behind me once more, then guided me to raise up on my knees. The squirting of lube from the bottle made me almost giddy. After six *long* years of teasing, we were finally about to do something about the sexual tension between us. "To answer your earlier question, I'm mad at myself."

"Why?"

Lachlan slid a finger into me and started moving it in and out of me. "Because some dumbass part of my brain has always worried that maybe I was secretly gay because of how much I love asses and anal sex. I was afraid to say yes to you because I didn't want to find that out about myself. And it's stupid, because there's nothing wrong with being gay, so why would it be a problem if I liked guys?"

"It's not."

"Exactly." He sighed with frustration before inserting another finger. "I feel like the world's biggest moron for turning you down for so many years. What we did in the shower was the most sexually satisfying experience I've ever had."

My ego purred at the compliment, especially since I knew how often he fucked. But I needed to reassure him more than I wanted to gloat. "Reframe your position on it, then. Tell yourself it was so good *because* of all the years of pent-up tension coming to a head. We were just engaging in some *really* glacially paced slow-burn foreplay. But now, you can move faster because I can take it."

He got the hint and added a third finger to stretch me. "Fuck, I'm going to be lucky if I don't explode the second I'm inside you. I'm so turned on I can't think straight."

"In my general experience, thinking straight is entirely overrated."

It was a relief when my joke earned a chuckle from him. "Are you saying I should think gay instead?"

"It can't hurt to give it a shot." I held my breath as he lined himself up with my entrance, then took his time sliding deep into me. "I hope you aren't planning to go that slow. I promise I can handle what you've got." To drive my point home, I shoved back hard against him to force him deeper.

"I've never done this without a condom before. I wasn't expecting it to make this much of a difference. *Holy shit.*"

"That makes two of us." I tightened around his buried length, earning me a swear as he pushed into me. "Now, show me what I've been missing. Don't hold back."

Thankfully, Lachlan didn't need to be told twice. He took a firm grip on my hips and gave me more reasons to be jealous of his ex-girlfriends. Once he realized I could take it, he plowed me hard and fast the way I liked it. He alternated between short and deep thrusts, driving me wild with lust as I finally got what I wanted.

"*Alessandro!*" The sound of my best friend crying out my name made it even better for me. It meant he wasn't imagining some girl as he fucked me; he was in the moment with me and still getting off on it.

"Give me more, Lachlan!" I cried out as he shifted

forward, allowing him to rut against me like a wild animal. "Fuck, yeah! Just like that!"

He didn't stop until he had fucked every thought out of my head, and then he kept going.

Chapter Four

LACHLAN

I HAD NEVER BEEN MORE TURNED on in my life. No matter how rough I got, Alessandro only grew louder as he cried out my name. He not only took what I gave him but begged me for more.

But it wasn't just that. Feeling the slick heat of a body welcoming me into it was a first for me, and I grew addicted to the unique experience. It was both a relief and an enormous turn-on to be intimate without barriers between us and not have to fear the consequences of an unwanted pregnancy. Because of my wealth, several women had hoped to trap me with that. As a result, it was a constant, low-key anxiety in the back of my mind whenever I hooked up.

However, Alessandro didn't care about my money *at all*. He had known me before I made my millions and treated me no differently than when I was the broke guy crashing on his couch who barely had two nickels to rub together. When so many of my other so-called "friends" acted like I was a bottomless ATM, it meant everything to me he didn't change. Hell, he still bought me beers and dinner sometimes when we went out instead of always expecting me to pay, since I was financially better off than him. More than anyone else, he had proven repeatedly that he only cared about me for who I was at my core and not the success I had become.

My mind was a jumble of realizations that got lost amidst the pleasure. Most surprising was that yet again, I didn't need to imagine I was with an Alessandra to enjoy myself. The fact that it was Alessandro under me actually made it better. It overwhelmed me as I raced to my climax faster than I wanted. But trying to slow down to drag out the experience was impossible. My hips drove into him, with the sound of our bodies connecting driving me wild. "Alessandro, I'm so close!"

Even more arousing were his moans and swears that pushed me to my limits. But I lost it when he cried out, "*Lachlan!*"

That did it for me. I buried myself to the hilt and came with a shout, thrusting until spent. It was such a powerful orgasm that it left me in a temporary daze. I needed a few moments to return to myself before I could pull out of him.

I was unprepared for what the sight of my cum leaking out of his pink hole would do to me. It filled me with wildfire that burned everything to ash, urging me to reach out and touch it as I whispered in awe, "Holy fuck, that's *so* sexy."

He glanced at me over his shoulder with a grin. "I'm assuming that means you like that?"

"More than I understand." I followed the trail down to his perineum. While I had always enjoyed shooting my load on my girlfriend, the satisfaction of seeing it seeping out of him was on a whole different level from that. What was it about my semen coming out of him that made me want to hold him down and fuck him harder?

"Are you ready to lose your mind?"

Distracted as I was, I didn't quite follow. "What do you mean?"

Instead of answering me with words, he tensed his muscles, forcing more of my cum to gush out of him. It aroused me beyond comprehension, driving me to slide my finger back into him to make more milky whiteness spill out of him. "Holy shit, I've never seen anything hotter in my life. If I could physically get hard again this fast, I'd be fucking you until you screamed right now."

"Please do whatever you can to make that happen," he groaned, pushing against me. "I'll beg you if it'll help."

It took a few moments before I registered he still hadn't orgasmed yet. While I could be selfish about a lot of things, that was never true in bed. If my partner hadn't climaxed, I wasn't finished. My autopilot kicked in as I withdrew my fingers and helped guide him onto his back. I moved up and kissed him with all the intense feelings my orgasm had left me with. I loved the way he tugged at my lower lip with his teeth as he tried to rub his hardness against me for some relief.

It felt like if I didn't get more of him, I'd lose my mind to madness. Driven by my urges, I began exploring his body with my lips and fingertips. He tilted his neck to give me better access, so I obliged him by kissing down it to his shoulder, then licking up it to suck on his earlobe.

I appreciated a nice pair of tits on a woman, especially when they were so large that it looked like they had an ass on their chest. But Alessandro was two aspirins on an ironing board compared to the women I had been with. It almost didn't seem worth giving my attention to, but my curiosity about how he'd react trumped my faulty reasoning. I swirled my tongue around one of his nipples, teasing it into a tight peak. When I pulled on it with my teeth, he swore with a loud gasp. His hands found purchase in my hair as I continued lavishing it with attention. I got more and more turned on by the way he squirmed under me with whimpers of need. If he kept doing that, it wouldn't take much longer before my arousal returned.

Switching to his left one, I used a hint of suction

before tweaking it with my teeth. At the same time, I toyed with the other. It was hot as fuck watching him getting worked up from the teasing.

"Please, Lachlan. I need you, so *please*!"

I moved down as I kissed my way down his faint happy trail. "Need me to do what?"

"Touch me!"

I reached down between us to cup his balls and give them a gentle squeeze. "Like this?" It was yet another unexpectedly arousing sensation.

"Lower!"

My hand snuck down to the ultimate temptation as I circled his hole. He was still wet and ready for me, which helped my dick get back in the game. "Here?"

He groaned when my fingers circled his entrance instead of penetrating him. "Yes, fuck me, damn it!"

I didn't expect my cock to respond to that, but it perked up with interest. It was a strange reaction considering I hated being bossed around, but I didn't have the presence of mind to think too deeply about it. I moved my hand away from him to jerk myself off, hoping to get myself hard enough to do what he wanted. "How bad do you want it?"

"If you don't hurry up and fuck me, I'll do it my damn self!"

The mental image of him fucking himself on his fingers as more of my cum came out of him got me closer to where I needed to be. "You wouldn't dare."

"Oh, not only will I dare, I'll do it and make you

sit there and watch." The challenging gleam in his eyes was sexier than it had any right to be. "Something tells me you'd much rather fill me up with your cum than waste it on your fist, though."

It was impressive that he knew all the right buttons to push to get my erection to return with full force. I lifted his hips up to allow me to reenter him. I skipped being cautious and took him hard and fast from the very beginning.

Alessandro arched up with a cry of ecstasy as his body rocked in sync with mine. He wrapped one of his legs around my waist for some leverage, but I hitched it higher to go deeper. I guided both of his legs over my shoulder as I shifted forward to hold his hips for leverage. He was nearly bent in half as I fucked him with a burning passion I didn't understand. It was liberating to be so unrestrained, especially because he was enjoying himself as much as I was.

The longer it went on, he almost sobbed with need as he jerked himself off. It aroused me even further to see how much he needed me in order to find release. I never would have imagined getting so turned on by watching my best friend pleasuring himself while I plowed him. When I shifted angles, he arched up with a gasp. "Right there! Oh, fucking right *there*, Lachlan!"

As I did my best to honor his request, every thrust to the same spot made him get louder. My curiosity got the better of me, so I reached down to grab his ass to see how he would react.

He didn't disappoint me. It was *so* satisfying hearing him shout as his body reacted to the pleasure. His cum almost hit his chest as it came out in spurts. I had no idea seeing him covered in his own semen would ignite my desires into a roaring blaze. It inspired me to pull out of him and straddle myself on top of him. He caught my drift because he reached out and started working my cock. Between that and imagining how it was going to look to see our releases commingling on his skin, my second orgasm crashed into me hard. I shot my load all over his stomach while crying out his name.

Seeing him covered in the evidence of our plea-sure made something deep within me purr with immense satisfaction. It was almost as if I had marked him as mine in a primitive sense. And shockingly, that thought felt really, *really* good. So good, in fact, that I wasn't ready to let that feeling go yet—if ever.

We stared at each other for a long moment as we attempted to recover our breath after our intense exertion. Before he could say anything, I gave in to my urge to lean down and kiss him. Lust had driven every other one, but this was gentle and an attempt to show my appreciation for how incredible he was at every-thing. I wasn't always the best at words, so I let my lips tell him what I didn't yet know how to express.

Chapter Five

ALESSANDRO

IT GAVE me whiplash at how fast we went from an animalistic fuck to Lachlan kissing me with tenderness. I hadn't prepared my heart for him to treat me so gently. It hit me twice as hard to have him kiss me like he loved me instead of being the guy he couldn't wait to rail again. I fought against the urge to cry from the unexpected gut punch of getting a taste of the only thing I had ever wanted more than him fucking me. I knew it would hurt like hell later, but I did my best to soak it all in, to make sure that single moment would last me a lifetime. It didn't matter how good of a lay I was; he would never give up women for me.

When he drew back, he looked at me with wonder. "*Wow.*"

Reminding myself to play it cool so I didn't weird

him out, I forced myself to give him a cocky grin. "My sentiments exactly."

The struggle not to cry became more difficult as he brushed my cheek with the thumb of his clean hand and said words I had always longed to hear. "I'm so sorry for making us wait six years for that."

Swallowing around the lump in my throat, I kept chanting to myself like a mantra, *Keep your shit together!* It took serious effort to play it off like it was nothing. "I'm glad you found out I was worth the wait."

"*More* than worth it." He reached down to caress my side as he looked at the cum splattered on my stomach. "I can't get over how fucking sexy it is to see you like this."

My ego delighted in the awe in his voice, but I had to downplay it to keep my heart from getting its hopes up. "I can't be the first person you've come on like this."

"No, but it's been a long time since it's been safe to do it."

Maybe it was the orgasmic haze, but his words didn't make sense. "Safe? What do you mean?"

"Hyacinthia ruined it for me."

I rolled my eyes at the reminder of one of his most notorious ex-girlfriends. "Why am I not surprised?"

"Because she's in the top tier of worst decisions I've made in my life."

"I won't disagree with you there. But I'm not seeing how she ruined this experience for you." I gestured at my stomach for emphasis.

He reached down to run his fingers through the cum, mixing our releases together. "Because I overheard her complaining to a friend about how her 'grand master plan' had been foiled. She had been so sure that by putting my cum inside herself that she'd get pregnant to force me to marry her. That was the real reason I broke up with her."

I was so outraged, no sound would come out when I attempted to protest. It took me several spluttering attempts before I could force out a full sentence. "What the actual fuck, Lachlan? One, what a fucking nightmare! Two, how am I only now hearing about this? That was four years ago!"

He shrugged as he kept swirling his fingers through the puddles on my skin. "Because I was too humiliated to admit that you were right about her after you begged me not to date her."

It didn't feel good to get confirmation that I had been correct. I reached up to guide him to look at me, allowing me to see the shame on his face. "It was never about me being right. All I wanted was for you to be okay."

"I know, which is why I felt like such a dumbass for not telling you about it." He sighed as he returned his gaze to the mess we had made. "After that, I was too scared someone else would try that tactic and be successful, which meant I could never do this kind of thing with a woman. And that sucked because it's incredibly sexy to mark your partner this way."

I was about to say something, but I interrupted myself with a gasp when he reached down to tease my hole again. There was so much longing in his voice when he said, "And seeing it coming out of you here made me damn near lose my mind." He inserted two fingers back inside me, making me whimper. "I can't stop remembering how hot it was to see it pouring out of you."

I trembled as he kept sliding his fingers in and out of me. "Oh, yeah?"

He added a third finger as he fucked me with them. "It made me want to hold you down and fill you up, just so I could watch it coming out of your pink hole again."

I shifted with a keen as my body responded to his dirty talk and teasing touch. His name escaped from me with a whimper as my dick did its best to rally for another go.

He stunned me when he withdrew his fingers, then coated them with our cum before slipping them back inside me. There was a possessive growl in his voice that gave me a semi as he said, "It makes you look like *mine*."

"That turned you on?"

"*So. Fucking. Much.*"

I cried out when he brushed against the spot that caused my dick to stand up at full attention. "Oh, *please!*"

He sought my prostate again, making me almost shout as he massaged it in a way that made me swear it wasn't his first time with a man. Every muscle in my body tensed in anticipation as I experienced the promising tingle about to overcome me. I only needed a little more to take me over the edge.

"Let me watch you come all over yourself, Alessandro."

Lachlan's authoritative growl did it for me. I arched off the bed as I made a bigger mess on my stomach by coming a second time while crying out his name. My breathing grew shaky as he pulled his fingers out of me to explore the latest addition to our masterpiece.

"You look so fucking *debauched*," he purred, giving me a whole new level of insight into his kinks.

I snorted at his praise as I glanced down at how fucking filthy I was. "Yeah, I look like the target of a *bukkake* circle jerk involving more than two guys."

There was a wild darkness in his blue eyes that sent a thrill through me. "Fuck, it makes me want to rub my dick in it and come again."

"Go ahead. Do it." Because I was a cocktease to my core, I reached down and swiped up some of our cum. I put on a show of sucking it off my finger as I stared him down with a dare.

He shuddered against me with a groan, "I think I had a third orgasm without coming. What the *fuck?*"

"I had no idea you were *that* into cum."

He had a dazed expression as he blinked at me in shock. "Neither did I."

"Clearly, I need to go clean up before you orgasm yourself into a coma." It stunned me when Lachlan honest-to-god pouted at the prospect of me washing off. "That means you're staying put until I'm done to avoid temptation."

He flopped onto his back with a heavy sigh. "That's probably for the best. I don't think either of us can handle what'll happen in the shower if I join you."

Although the last thing I felt like doing was moving, my need to clean up was stronger than my sloth instincts. I arched an eyebrow when I glimpsed myself in his bathroom mirror. We had certainly made a fucking mess.

As I got into the shower, part of me was sad I had to wash off the evidence of how good it had felt to *finally* get what I wanted. Well, *mostly* get what I wanted. Hooking up with Lachlan was part of my fantasy, but I wanted him for keeps. His reactions to fucking me gave me more hope that maybe it wasn't as far-fetched of a possibility as I previously thought. I never would have imagined he'd get *that* turned on by *cum*. What straight guy was into that?

Blanking my mind before I got myself spun up, I took my time rinsing off before I used the bathroom and returned to his room. To my surprise, Lachlan wasn't there. Instead of worrying about it, I pulled back the covers and crawled under them to get in bed. There was no way I was driving home after what we had done.

Closing my eyes with a sigh, I focused on the bone-deep satisfaction humming through me after our encounter. It had been so incredible, I didn't know what I was going to do if he didn't want a repeat experience. But after being his friend for six years, I couldn't imagine him and his intense sex drive being okay with it being a one-and-done. Maybe my luck hadn't run out yet and I'd get another chance to be with him.

Lachlan returned with two bottles of water. He handed me one before getting back into bed with me. "I figured we both needed this."

"Good call." My tired body didn't want to move, but I sat up to take a drink. "Thanks."

He took several swallows before putting the cap back on the bottle. "Are you up for one more experiment tonight?"

"As long as it doesn't involve my dick or any effort, sure." I grinned when he laughed at my answer. "You officially wore me out."

"I'm curious what it would be like to hold someone who is almost as tall as me."

Lachlan's long list of girlfriends had all been significantly shorter than him, but that wasn't surprising when he was six four. I struggled to hide my grin at his request. "Are you asking if you can spoon me?"

He gave a mock sniff of disdain. "Yes, if you want to call it something so juvenile."

"Would you rather me tease you about wanting to cuddle-wuddle with little ol' me?" I asked in a baby voice that made him laugh hard. "Or would you prefer if I joke about you wanting to snuggle me like your favorite teddy bear?"

"That's real cute, Alessandro."

"Hey, I made you laugh. Joking aside, being your little spoon sounds great."

He tilted his head as he looked at me with curiosity. "Does it?"

I cursed myself for my slipup in not being more specific. Trying to cover my ass, I hurried to add, "It does for tonight. I'm wiped out and ready to crash for the night."

"That makes two of us." He stretched, allowing me to appreciate his beautiful body. "Damn, I can't remember the last time I felt *this* satisfied after being with someone."

"I guess that's the difference between hooking up

with your best friend versus some random girl you met at a party."

He nodded in agreement. "Tonight was eye-opening in a lot of different ways."

"Is that good or bad?" It was hard to judge from his tone.

"I'm pretty sure it's good." He finished his water and set it on his nightstand before getting up to shut off the lights and returning to bed. "I don't have enough of a brain left right now to brood over it."

Snickering at his comment, I chucked my bottle over to his nightstand and missed it by a country mile. "Oops. Sorry."

"Don't worry about it." He waited for me to roll over before he scooted behind me and pulled me into his embrace.

After longing for him to hold me that way for six *long* years, it was even better than I had imagined. Melting against him with a soft sigh, I cherished the moment that was everything I had ever wanted.

"This is nice," he murmured, hugging me a little tighter to his chest.

It was an understatement, but I didn't feel up to correcting him. "Mm-hmm."

He turned me into a quivering puddle when he kissed the back of my shoulder. "Good night, Alessandro."

It was an intimate gesture that I would hold on to for the rest of my life. I could barely speak through my exhaustion and emotional state, but I forced myself to mumble, "G'night."

As we settled into silence, I was too tired to think. Instead, I drifted into a dreamless sleep, because there was no better dream than the reality of being his, even if it was only for one night.

Chapter Six

LACHLAN

I WOKE up with Alessandro sprawled out on top of me like a weighted blanket. The strangeness of it took a moment to process. Normally, I had a smaller woman with her breasts pressed against me as she slept. While I had a broader frame than him, I was barely two inches taller than him. As I held him around his waist, my half-asleep instincts appreciated his soft skin. Everything about being with him made my lizard brain happy on a primitive level I didn't understand.

Last night with him had been an eye-opening experience as I tapped into a side of my sexuality I hadn't realized existed. Considering how much I loved the gentle curves of a woman, I never imagined I'd get so turned on by a guy. Not only that, but who knew fucking a man would be so hot and satisfying? But was it any guy or just Alessandro? Something told me I wouldn't have had the same reaction to Baxley if I had hooked up with him, though. I probably still would have gotten off because my dick wasn't picky about my partners, but I bet it never would have stirred the same kinds of feelings within me.

No, the primitive part of my soul only purred at the thought of making Alessandro mine. It had the strangest urge to mark him with my cum like an animal claiming its mate. The memory of seeing it dripping from his pink hole made my cock spring to life, hoping to have a repeat experience. It was a mystery to me why that was such an affecting thing for me. All I could figure was that my semen had become hazardous around women hoping to turn it into a child. With him, I didn't have to worry about that, which was arousing in its own right. I could be as filthy as I wanted with him without consequence, because he had always accepted me as I was.

Unable to resist, my hand snuck down to cop a feel of his glorious ass. It made him rock against me with a sleepy murmur. I continued caressing the plump swell of his mounds, getting more aroused as I felt him grow hard against my hip. When I dipped my fingers between his cheeks to tease his pucker, that earned me a groan as he finally stirred.

"I'm going to be *so* pissed at you if you woke me up with teasing and aren't planning to follow through on this," he grumbled.

I reached down to guide his hand to wrap around

my erection as evidence that I was more than prepared to act. "Does this answer your question?"

He gave it a few pumps that got me all hot and bothered. "It sure does."

Rolling Alessandro onto his back, I threw off the covers and grabbed the lube from my nightstand. I wasted no time in plunging my slick fingers into him as I readied him to move on to the best part.

He shifted under me with a sigh. "You have my permission to start more mornings this way."

"I need to see you ride me." An interesting rumble escaped me at the thought. "*Hard.*"

"Yes, sir," he moaned, arching up under my touch.

As soon as I withdrew my fingers, he reversed our positions. However, he surprised me by turning away from me as he straddled over me.

"What are you doing?"

"Indulging what I imagine is one of your favorite positions." He rubbed my cock between his ass cheeks as he teased me. "Or are you seriously telling me you've never done reverse cowboy before?"

I took a deep breath to steady myself in the face of an unexpected offer. "Never with anal."

"Well, then you're in for a real treat today." He leaned forward and spread his cheeks apart to reveal temptation. I couldn't resist tapping my dick against his hole a few times to mark his skin with my precum. "Let me show you what you've been missing."

I guided my tip into him, then watched with

growing lust as I slid deep inside him. Being intimately buried in his slick heat without having to use a condom was incredibly arousing. And from the angle he gifted me, that meant I could also watch my release spilling out of him as soon as I came, which turned me on even more.

He worked up to a slow bounce, letting me savor the sight of his perfect bubble butt on full display. It jiggled every time it connected with my body, driving me wild with lust. I reached out and grabbed two handfuls of his plump ass and helped guide his movements. It was so fucking sexy watching my dick pumping in and out of him as he rode me hard. I hadn't thought anything would be hotter than what we did yesterday, but I was thrilled to be wrong about that.

My hips ceaselessly drove into him, earning me the most delightful moans and swears as he rocked my world. It got even better when he braced himself on my thighs to fuck himself harder on my cock.

I appreciated the gentle slope of his back as he arched it in pleasure. My hands migrated up to his hips, gripping them hard as I lost myself in the ecstasy echoing between our bodies. But I couldn't resist alternating between caressing his ass and grabbing it. It made him get louder as we rocked together. Every time he called out to me, I became more aroused by the experience.

I could feel my orgasm building up inside, and the

anticipation of getting to watch what happened from that angle made it more exciting. Pulling him down hard as I pushed in as far as I could, I came with a shout. He slowly moved off me, letting me see my cum dripping out of him and down my dick. It was hot as hell, but I wanted more.

Alessandro wasn't about to stop there. He moved forward onto his hands and knees, leaving only the tip of my cock in him. As I slipped out, my semen trickled out of him until he forced out more.

The sight of it pouring out of him broke something loose inside of me. Without thinking, I moved into a position that allowed me to act on the strange instinct burning within me. It demanded I do what I would have once considered unthinkable. I leaned forward to lick the trail of cum from his balls up to his perineum. More of my release came out of him as he tensed with a gasp of shock. It compelled me to run my tongue up to his hole.

I could hear the shock in his voice as he exclaimed in disbelief at my actions. But unless he told me to stop, I intended to keep going. Rimming was on my list of things I had long fantasized about doing. However, none of my previous girlfriends had ever let me do it because they thought it was too gross. I spread his cheeks further apart to allow me to suck on his pucker and draw out more of my cum. It turned me on even further as I slid my tongue into him, testing the limits of what he would tolerate.

Alessandro braced himself on his forearms as he gasped, "Holy *fuck*, Lachlan!"

I heard the pleasure in his voice, so I kept going. Alternating between tonguing him as deep as I could, flicking my tongue against his hole, and sucking at it, it was heavenly living out my ultimate fantasy. The taste of my cum made it even hotter as I got worked up all over again, not caring about the lube. He trembled under me with desperate cries, but I didn't relent.

"Fuck, fuck, fuck, fucking *fuck*!" He grew louder with each exclamation as he rocked against my face. "I'm gonna come so—*why the fuck are you stopping?*"

"Not stopping, promise." I wiped the mess off my lips and chin on the back of my hand. Guiding him to turn over, I spread his legs further apart as I settled between them. The burning need inside me that hungered for things I didn't understand licked along the length of his erection before I swirled my tongue to clean off the precum. When that didn't turn me off, I took him into my mouth and sucked on as much of his dick as I could.

His hands scrambled for purchase in my hair as he all but shouted. It made me want to see what happened if I put my fingers back inside him while I did my best to blow him. He squirmed under me as I pushed against the bump I had figured out last time was his prostate. As he came in my mouth, I swallowed his release, shocked by how much it aroused me to have him do that. I was certainly learning all kinds of new and surprising things about myself.

It made my erection return with full force. I lifted his hips as I pressed the tip against his entrance once more. "Can I?"

"*Please!*"

It was all the permission I needed to reenter him. To my surprise, I didn't start another fast and furious fuck. I took my time as I rocked our bodies together as I caressed him all over, hoping my touch would convey what being intimate with him meant to me. He arched up with soft moans, hitching one of his legs over my hip. I hiked it higher as I pumped in and out of him. It felt like I was making love to him, especially when he pulled me down closer and trailed kisses along my jaw, up to my ear. His breathy whimpers sent shivers of wildfire raging through me as his body welcomed me deeper.

"I want you so much," I accidentally groaned, since my flimsy filter had taken a back seat to the pleasure.

He reached down to encourage his half-hard dick to get fully erect again. "Yes!"

"Want to make you mine so bad." Those words also escaped from me without my permission, but they weren't a lie.

"Do it!"

I wasn't sure how to make it happen, but I knew it would require more than using my cum to claim him.

It was an urge from somewhere deep inside me I didn't understand. But as I kept racing toward my climax, I took his hardness in hand. "Does the thought of being mine really arouse you this much?"

He didn't answer with anything more than a needy keen as I tried to jerk him off. His muscles tensed as his cries hit a fevered pitch before he exploded all over my fist and his stomach with a shout. The sight took me over the edge. I came with a satisfied moan and a full-body shudder, thrusting until I was spent.

Pulling out, I allowed myself the thrill of watching my cum seeping out of him and down his crack to make the sheets wet under him. It added another layer to my satisfaction that I couldn't quite explain. However, it made me realize with shock that I wasn't interested in a one-night stand with my best friend. But that didn't answer the most important question: Did I want a friends-with-benefits situation, or did I want to date my best friend for real?

Chapter Seven

ALESSANDRO

I MUST HAVE COME SO MUCH that I lost what little mind I possessed. Or maybe I had orgasmed myself into a parallel universe where my best friend was gay and got off on rimming me like a pro and sucking my dick. How else could I explain what Lachlan had done?

As overwhelmed as I was, I barely registered when he left to go brush his teeth and wash his face. All I could do was lie still and wonder how he had so masterfully flipped everything around on me with being sexually adventurous. His skilled tongue would have made me even more jealous of his ex-girlfriends if I had the energy leftover after our morning romp.

When he returned, he brought a warm washcloth to tend to me. It was a level of thoughtfulness that tugged on my heartstrings and made it *really* hard not to feel things for him I wasn't allowed. It became harder when he got back in bed with me, then gave me a sweet kiss. I had to do something—*anything*—to stop myself from drowning in love, so I did what I did best: act like a smart-ass. "Mm, who knew making out with a minty-fresh toothbrush was so hot?"

He chuckled as he stretched out next to me and propped his head up on his hand. "I figured you'd prefer that over tasting cum and lube first thing in the morning."

"Ha, shows how well you know me. That's my preferred way to flavor my coffee."

It was cute how he scrunched up his nose. "I'll pretend you didn't say that."

"Oh, so *that* grosses you out but not rimming me like you've been gay your whole life?" I snorted in amusement. "I'm starting to think you aren't nearly as straight as you claim to be."

He once again caught me off guard. "That makes two of us."

My eyebrows furrowed with concern. "What's going on with you? Because I don't know how we went from 'It would be funny if we fooled around in the shower' to you eating my ass like it's your favorite meal."

His gaze shifted to travel over my body as he tried to explain himself. "I've always been curious about rimming someone, but the few women I've asked wouldn't let me since they said it was too dirty. And that was *without* cum and lube being involved."

His answer didn't surprise me. "I'll admit it shocked me you did it after we had gone that far instead of starting there."

"You didn't stop me, though."

"No, you stopped yourself." We both laughed. "And if you'll recall, I was *very* upset until you flipped me over to blow me. Speaking of which, what the fuck was *that* about?"

He shrugged. "No clue. I wasn't thinking; I was just reacting on instinct. Something in me wanted to taste your pleasure, so I went straight to the source."

"Taste my pleasure?" My eyebrows arched up at his choice of phrasing. "Considering how down and dirty you are, that's a surprisingly poetic way to say you wanted to drink my cum like a milkshake."

"You have a point." I loved how he laughed hard at my reaction until his expression turned pensive. "It's weird that didn't gross me out, isn't it?"

"Not gonna lie—it's a bit strange, yeah." I didn't want to make him feel self-conscious about something so amazing, so I hurried to expand on my thoughts. "But it's also fucking incredible you're open-minded enough to be this chill about exploring your sexuality. You've always been laid-back about stuff, so it makes sense it applies to this as well. When you think of it in those terms, it's actually not surprising you're reacting this way."

"True." He was silent as he continued mulling over the situation. "What's odd is I didn't have a

'Huh, I didn't hate it' reaction to what we did. It was 'Fuck, I *loved* that' instead."

I couldn't stop myself from teasing him. "Are you saying I'm like a fun carnival ride you want to go on again and again?"

His blue eyes lit up with excitement. "I'd be down for future rides for sure."

"Does that mean you also want to gorge yourself on my cotton candy fluff while you're at it?"

He snorted at my choice of phrase. "Is that what we're calling it now?"

"Can you think of a more appropriate sticky carnival treat to use in this analogy instead? Because caramel candy apple doesn't have quite the same imagery."

"Fair enough." A hint of fire in his gaze heated me up. "I'd be lying if I said I wasn't eager for another taste."

My hopes took off like a hot-air balloon, but I yanked them back down to earth. Lachlan didn't mean it that way, and I couldn't afford to let myself get excited about it. We would never be more than friends fooling around at best. "You'll have to wait until the stand reopens, because we're fresh out of cotton candy at the moment after an unexpected rush on it this morning."

We both cracked up before he shifted topics. "You never answered my question earlier."

Nothing immediately came to mind. "Sorry, but I

only have two remaining brain cells left after what we just did. You need to be more specific."

He pinned me under his blue gaze, making it harder to breathe. "I asked you if the thought of being mine aroused you that much?"

My heart thudded in my chest. It was a question I wasn't prepared to answer. "I don't think it's fair to ask when you had your dick buried in my ass and I was ready to shout, 'Yes,' to anything that would make me come."

"What about now that we're both in a calmer state of mind?"

I tried to deflect from the uncomfortable subject. "I'm pretty sure it's not applicable now."

His eyebrow quirked up, which was hot as hell. "I disagree."

"Oh?"

"It's not only applicable—it's a critical piece of information I need to know."

I stared at him in confusion. "Why?"

"I can't decide without knowing."

It gave me a case of emotional whiplash at how fast we went from "Ha-ha, funny" to an "Oh, *shit*" conversation. Well, *that* certainly wasn't the turn I hoped our post-fuck canoodling would take.

Chapter Eight

ALL TRACES of good humor faded as the color seemed to drain from Alessandro's face. He stared at me with eyes wide in fear, his voice shaking as he asked, "What decision?"

"How we move forward." My answer didn't ease the worried expression on his face. It was upsetting to see him anxious because of me. "If this was merely you humoring my whim, that's one thing. If you're interested in actually being mine in the long-term sense, that's something else."

He blinked as he tried to process what I had said. How had I never noticed how beautiful his eyelashes were before? "What are you saying?"

I laid all my cards on the table. "I'm asking if this was a one-time thing, a friends-with-benefits situation, or if you're interested in dating me for real?"

A fascinating range of emotions flitted across

Alessandro's face before he spluttered an incredulous reaction. "Wait—are you—you can't seriously be saying—there's *no way* you're asking if we can be *boyfriends*!"

"Why not?"

It was hard not to laugh at his baffled expression. "Because men don't shift from being straight to wanting a boyfriend just because they got their rocks off with a guy once!"

I couldn't resist being pedantic. "In fairness, it was more than once."

"Fine, one *night*."

"And one morning, too."

He huffed with a consternated scowl. "You actually expect me to believe your pendulum swung from 'super straight' to 'really fucking gay' that fast?"

"While I was cleaning up in the bathroom earlier, I took an objective look at the facts." I started counting my points on my fingers. "There's nobody I trust or care about more than you. We both would do anything to help each other. And it was by far the hottest sex of my life."

He couldn't stop himself from grinning. "Yeah, it was definitely a five-alarm fire of red-hot sexiness."

I still had more reasons to list. "Not to mention it was fucking *liberating* to not have some part of my brain spending the entire time worrying you might use sex against me like I do when I'm with my girlfriends. You weren't fucking me for my money, or to use me to get a leg up in society, or to get knocked up by me to cash in on my fortune. You were with me because you like me for me. You also didn't judge me for being into so-called 'dirty' things like my exes always did. That was huge for me."

"That's all well and good, but that doesn't mean you want everything else dating me would entail."

I couldn't resist challenging his assertion. "And what other part of dating do you think I would object to?"

He floundered at my question. "I don't know. The non-sex parts of it all?"

"Do you honestly believe that?" I scoffed at the ridiculous notion. "One of the biggest downsides of having a girlfriend has always been spending less time with you."

He rubbed his hand over his eyes before ruffling his hair with a groan. "Please don't say things that could be misconstrued as romantic. My heart can't handle it right now."

His intriguing reaction hadn't been the one I expected. Had I really been so blind I hadn't noticed his teasing was based on genuine feelings? "I don't think you're misconstruing anything."

"What do you mean?"

"When I have a shitty day, you're the person I go to in order to make it better. If I have a good day, I want to hang out with you to turn it into an awesome one. Whenever I'm being a dumbass, you're the only one who cares about me enough to call me on my shit. If I don't know what the hell I'm doing, you're the one who tells me how to fix things. No matter what the situation is, my instinct has always been to seek you out because you've always made everything better."

He blinked at me with a stunned expression but said nothing.

"Hanging out, watching a movie together after dinner, and talking after it's over is a pretty typical date night with the women I've been with. But it also describes what you and I have been doing for the past six years."

He rubbed his temples as he collected his thoughts. "Yeah, but it's different with us."

"Only because I was too stupid to see what was right in front of me. Since the beginning, I always thought being your friend was the best thing that ever happened to me. But you've made me realize being your boyfriend would be even better."

"But you're *straight*."

I got the impression he was protesting more for my sake, so I needed to put a stop to it. "Do straight men give other men rim jobs? Or suck their dicks?"

"Well, no, but——"

"Then I guess I'm not straight, am I?"

He huffed in a cute way. "It doesn't work like that!"

"It works however I want it to. I don't give a shit

about labels. Whether I'm straight, bi, or a yousexual, none of that matters to me. All I care about is being with you."

A slow grin spread over his face. "Mesexual, huh?"

"It's a little easier to say than Alessandrosexual." I caressed his cheek as I held his gaze. "Whatever I am, I know I want everything with you. I'll freely admit I want more mind-blowing sex. But last night made me realize the hanging out and cuddling parts of being with you are something I want, too. I want *you*, and not just because your ass is so perfect, it would win a blue ribbon at the carnival fair."

That finally broke his weird headspace as he cracked up at my last comment. It took him a few moments to recover his composure enough to ask, "You honestly mean that, don't you?"

"I can't think of anything better than dating my best friend."

"Who also has a sweet ass," he added with a playful grin.

"It's a nice bonus prize, but it's not the primary reason. I like who I am around you, and the way you make me feel. I want to experience that goodness all the time. Plus, it'll make copping a feel way less creepy if it's officially sanctioned by our relationship."

It was getting harder for him to smother his grin. "You might have a point."

"My only regret is waiting so long to give in to

your teasing." I scowled at the thought. "We could have been having this kind of fun years ago if I hadn't been so dense."

"In your defense, Baxley has also flirted with you a ton. We're all a bunch of perverts who can't resist a good punchline. Of course you wouldn't take either of us seriously."

"But it's more than that." I frowned as I tried to put my feelings into words. "It's like I stubbornly wore blinders that focused exclusively on liking women and refused to consider the possibility I might like men, too. Why? Was I really scared to discover guys can also have nice asses I want to enjoy? Why would I fear that when I don't have a problem with anyone being gay?"

He gave me a sympathetic look. "Sexuality is complicated. Previously, you were content with where you fell on the spectrum at that point as a straight man. If it feels right for you to change now, that's perfectly fine, too. We don't have to be only one thing our entire lives. As long as you're comfortable and happy, that's all that matters. Labels are secondary."

I appreciated his attempt to console me, but I persisted. "But being with you was *incredible*. I should have realized sooner when you're always the person I have the most fun being around. It never occurred to me you could be more than just a platonic soul mate best friend. And now, it seems like the most obvious thing in the world. I don't know how the hell I missed it for so long."

Both of his eyebrows arched up in shock. "Wait, are you seriously already upgrading me to *romantic* soul mate status?"

"That depends on whether you want to be my boyfriend. You haven't officially agreed yet."

"You truly want to be with me? Like, go out on dates, saying, 'I love you,' spending the holidays with each other's families, having schmoopy anniversary celebrations, and someday saying, 'I do,' in front of all our friends and loved ones? That's what you want with me?"

"All of that, and more. I want to love you and be your everything, Alessandro."

His eyelashes fluttered as he looked at me in awe. "You already are. You have been since the beginning."

"Then, it sounds like we should make it official." I took his hand in mine and brought it up to my lips to kiss. "Will you be my boyfriend?"

"The only thing that would make me happier is someday being your husband." He guided me closer to give me an enthusiastic kiss. "The answer is yes."

When we kissed again, I knew with startling clarity that Alessandro was the one for me. Instead of regretting how long it took me to realize the perfect partner was in front of me all along, I celebrated that we could move forward together into our future lifetime of happiness.

Epilogue

AFTER BREAKFAST, Lachlan and I went out to his pool to lounge on his rainbow unicorn and pink flamingo floats. I soaked up the warm sun as I basked in the glory of my best friend now being my boyfriend. I didn't know how I had gotten so lucky, but I was over the moon with happiness. But I wasn't sure how he felt about broadcasting the change in our status from friends to dating. "Do you want to tell Baxley and Callahan when they come over?"

"Yeah, why wouldn't we?" It felt great that he reacted to my question like it was an absurd concern. "I'm not ashamed. Besides, over half of our other friends already assumed we were dating. We'll be confirming their suspicions more than announcing something new to them."

I looked over at him with surprise. "Huh. You

always seemed oblivious to their opinions in that regard."

"This is going to make me sound like a huge asshole, but I don't care what they think."

I grinned at his reaction. "You're right, that kinda makes you sound like an asshole."

He shrugged it off. "I've never lived my life caring what other people think about me and what I do. The only person's opinion I care about is yours."

"And yet you didn't think you loved me."

"Luckily for me, you have a secret weakness for dumbasses in denial. It would have been a disaster otherwise." He gestured at Baxley and Callahan approaching with a wave. "And speaking of dumbass disasters, look who finally showed up."

"We figured if we came too early, you'd still be fucking like sex-starved bunnies trying to make up for lost time." Baxley grinned as he stripped down to his swimming trunks, then cannonballed in with a huge splash.

"I was prepared to walk in on the two of you going at it," Callahan added as he jumped in next, spraying more water. "I've gotta say, I'm a little disappointed you're out here just chilling."

"Are you that hard up for free porn?" I laughed as I kicked some water in his direction. "Although, I guess that's good news for Baxley that you're taking an interest in watching two guys fucking."

He pushed his hair back with a laugh. "Why would that be good news for him?"

Floating up behind his best friend, Baxley caressed Callahan's body, earning a shocked noise from him. "Because maybe it'll inspire you to practice with me for real."

He rolled his eyes at the predictable response. "Are you so desperate for sex that you have to fuck *me* to get some action?"

"No, but my hard-on is *very* interested in getting more intimately acquainted with you." Baxley tugged on the shell of Callahan's ear with his teeth, earning an interesting noise out of his captive. "I'd love to show you everything you're missing out on."

"Sorry, but a sore ass isn't the great selling point you think it is." Callahan swam out of his friend's hold.

I frowned at the interaction. "Damn, I really thought you'd hook up last night."

Baxley shrugged. "It wasn't for lack of trying."

Callahan changed the subject. "So, what happened after we left yesterday?"

"We need explicit details," Baxley added. "Don't leave anything out."

I couldn't resist the easy punchline. "You want the blow-by-blow replay?"

His eyes lit up with excitement. "Hell yeah I do!"

"Let's leave it at I learned a very valuable lesson

about why I was so stupid for waiting to give in," Lachlan diplomatically answered.

Baxley swam closer with an interested hum. "And what are you planning on doing with your new knowledge? Maybe a little more experimenting, perhaps?"

Callahan dunked Baxley into the water, laughing when his friend popped up to the surface with a splutter.

Wiping the water from his eyes and slicking back his hair, Baxley scowled. "What the hell was that for?"

"To cool you off before you did something stupid, like hitting on Lachlan by offering to experiment with him next."

"Why? Would that make you jealous if I did?"

It was adorable how Callahan huffed in irritation. "I'm not saying that."

Baxley moved closer to him, but his prey escaped. "Then what are you saying if not, 'Stay away from him. You're mine,' hmm?"

Callahan splashed at his friend to force him away when he tried to close in on him again. "Stop trying to put words in my mouth."

"Would you rather me put my dick in it instead?" Baxley snickered at the aghast reaction his question earned him. "I can promise you'll enjoy it."

"Take it from me: the only regret you'll have is waiting so long to act," Lachlan assured him. It felt amazing to hear him asserting how much he wished he had given in to me sooner.

Callahan fussed about being ganged up on. "Right, but to what end? You fuck once and go back to being friends like nothing ever happened? I can't do that."

"No, we're dating now." It filled my heart with joy that Lachlan announced our new relationship status without any hesitation or shame. That was so much more than I had ever dared to hope.

Callahan's jaw dropped in shock. "*Seriously?*"

Baxley never missed an opportunity to drag the conversation into the gutter. "Damn, Alessandro. You must have some serious talent in the bedroom to make Mr. Hetero switch teams permanently."

I grinned wolfishly at him. "If you need any tips, we can talk later."

Callahan got us back on topic. "Wait, so you're *actually* dating? Like, boyfriends in love and not just friends with benefits?"

Lachlan's contented smile lifted my spirits even further. "Yes, and I couldn't be happier. I was a fool for refusing to see what's been in front of me for so long because I was too scared to take that chance."

"Hint, hint," Baxley added because he was allergic to subtlety.

Callahan ignored him. "In that case, congrats. You're perfect for each other, so I'm happy for you both."

Baxley swam up behind him to embrace his best friend. "And hopefully, you're a little inspired to see where things could go if you gave in to our sexual tension. After all, if it worked out for them, why wouldn't it work out for us?"

"It's never going to happen when I'm a relationship guy and the mere thought of being someone's boyfriend gives you hives." Callahan escaped his grasp and jumped out to sit on the edge of the pool with his legs in the water.

Taking pity on our friend, I spoke in his defense. "That's true with everyone else, but something tells me that he'd be different with you."

"You'll never know if you don't take a chance." Lachlan reached over and tugged my float close enough to hold my hand. He brought it up to his lips to kiss the back of it. "I'm glad I did."

"I'm glad we both did." I blew him a flirty kiss. "And I look forward to showing you how happy you make me later."

He squeezed my hand with a smile. "And for the rest of our lives."

It didn't get any better than having your best friend be the greatest love of your life.

hotter
than hot

SUNTASTIC FUN ☀ BOOK TWO

ARIELLA ZOELLE

SUNTASTIC FUN ☀ BOOK TWO

ARIELLA ZOELLE

Chapter One

BAXLEY

I WAS a shameless flirt who talked a big game and had a reputation for never being with the same person twice. As a result, my straight best friend had written me off as a commitmentphobe, which couldn't be further from the truth. Callahan would die of shock if he knew I had been living like a celibate monk for the past three years. The ultimate irony was that I couldn't commit to a partner because I was already in a long-term commitment to *him*—he just didn't know it. And the worst part was it was my own damn fault for falling into the pattern of hitting on him as a joke he'd laugh off. I couldn't help it when the teasing banter was the best foreplay I could get under the circumstances.

Our friend, Alessandro, was in the same situation as me, where he was hopelessly in love with his oblivious, straight best friend, Lachlan. After yesterday's joking around in the pool, the lucky bastard got to live out my fantasy of indulging his bicuriousity with a blow job in the shower. It probably led to even more sexual explorations after we left last night. While I was happy Alessandro had made his dreams come true, I still felt the ugly burn of jealousy.

Since it was summer and Lachlan was loaded with a sweet beach house, pool, and more money than God, his place was our de facto hangout spot. I picked up Callahan on the way over, who was precious in his white tank and blue swimming trunks. Because of his fair Irish skin, he slathered up with SPF-1000 to prevent him from burning to a crisp under the scorching sun. It was my favorite time of year, because being outside always darkened his cute little freckles that dotted his shoulders. I loved how his auburn hair looked like fire in the sunlight and how his green eyes sparkled with laughter.

Yeah, I had it *really* fucking bad for him. *Ugh.*

I punched in the code to open the gate to Lachlan's beach house—which was a bit of a misnomer. It was a massive mansion with red Spanish terra-cotta tiles he'd bought with his millions he had made being a finance bro. While I liked to tease him about it, I had a ton of respect for him. Money almost always changed people, but Lachlan was the same guy he was before he made it big. He was down-to-earth, laid-back, and loved a dirty joke. With his broad build and hot-guy-next-door good looks, he never had any shortage of women. The money factor complicated things, because he kept attracting all the wrong kinds who only wanted him for his bank account. I wished he'd do us all the favor and fall in love with Alessandro, who didn't care if he had ten dollars or ten million to his name.

When I parked, we grabbed our bags from my car with our change of clothes for later after our pool fun.

"Do you think they fucked?" Callahan asked as we headed inside.

"I'm going to be really disappointed if they didn't."

He laughed as we made our way out back to the massive pool. Lachlan was sprawled out over his rainbow unicorn float. He was a gorgeous god of a man with his well-chiseled muscles, broad frame, tan skin, and blond hair.

Alessandro soaked up the sun on the flamingo float nearby. He was smaller in build, with dark hair and bronze skin, which stood out in stark contrast to the pink bird he was lounging on. They both were so delightfully dorky.

In true Lachlan fashion, he greeted us by busting our balls. "And speaking of dumbass disasters, look who finally showed up."

"We figured if we came too early, you'd still be fucking like sex-starved bunnies trying to make up for lost time." Grinning, I dropped my bag and stripped down to my swimming trunks, then cannonballed in with a huge splash to soak them both.

Thankfully, I resurfaced in time to watch Callahan strip off his tank and bare his lithe body. I ached to memorize every curve of him with my lips and fingertips. "I was prepared to walk in on the two of you going at it." He followed my lead with a second cannonball attack. "I've gotta say, I'm a little disappointed you're out here just chilling."

"Are you that hard up for free porn?" Alessandro playfully kicked some water in Callahan's direction for the smart-ass comment. "Although, I guess that's good news for Baxley that you're taking an interest in watching two guys fucking."

Callahan drove me wild by slicking his red hair away from his eyes. "Why would that be good news for him?"

It was too tempting of an invitation to resist. I swam up behind him and held him in an embrace while caressing his sides, earning me a cute squawk of surprise. "Because maybe it'll inspire you to practice with me for real." *Oh, to be so lucky…*

"Are you so desperate for sex that you have to fuck *me* to get some action?"

You have no *idea*, I thought with a woeful inner sigh. I had three years of pent-up lust I was dying to satiate with the object of my obsession. Instead, I had to play it cool. "No, but my hard-on is *very* interested in getting more intimately acquainted with you." I tugged on the shell of Callahan's ear with my teeth, earning an interesting noise out of my captive. "I'd love to show you everything you're missing out on."

"Sorry, but a sore ass isn't the great selling point you think it is." It was hard not to pout when he swam out of my loose hold.

Alessandro frowned. "Damn, I really thought you'd hook up last night."

I fucking wish. "It wasn't for lack of trying."

It didn't surprise me when Callahan changed the subject. "So, what happened after we left yesterday?"

"We need explicit details," I added. "Don't leave anything out."

Alessandro smirked. "You want the blow-by-blow replay?"

Since I had to live vicariously through him getting what I wanted, I wasn't willing to turn down that kind of offer. "Hell yeah I do!"

"Let's leave it at I learned a very valuable lesson about why I was so stupid for waiting to give in," Lachlan diplomatically answered. Out of the four of us, he was the most reserved, so it was a surprisingly honest response.

I swam closer to him with an interested hum. "And what are you planning on doing with your new knowledge? Maybe a little more experimenting, perhaps?"

It caught me off guard when Callahan pounced on me from behind to dunk me. I popped up to the surface with a splutter, wiping the water from my eyes as I pushed my dark hair back. "What the hell was that for?"

The cute bastard was entirely unrepentant about his actions, which only made me love him even more. "To cool you off before you did something stupid, like hitting on Lachlan by offering to experiment with him next."

Now *that* was an interesting response. "Why? Would that make you jealous if I did?" *Please say yes.*

It was adorable how he huffed in irritation. "I'm not saying that."

I moved closer, but he darted off before I could catch him. That left me no choice but to use my words to reach him. "Then what are you saying if not, 'Stay away from him. You're mine,' hmm?"

He splashed at me to force distance between us when I closed in on him again. "Stop trying to put words in my mouth."

"Would you rather me put my dick in it instead?" I snickered at the aghast reaction my question earned me. It was too easy to rile him up. "I can promise you'll enjoy it."

I never expected Lachlan to encourage Callahan on the matter. "Take it from me: the only regret you'll have is waiting so long to act."

Some of Callahan's playfulness faded away as his eyebrows furrowed with frustration. "Right, but to what end? You fuck once and go back to being friends like nothing ever happened? I can't do that."

I wanted to tell him that if he ever agreed to be in my bed, I would never let him out again. But I lost the opportunity when Lachlan stunned me with his announcement. "No, we're dating now."

Callahan's jaw dropped in shock. "*Seriously?*"

Oh, that *so* wasn't fair. It was one thing for Alessandro and Lachlan to be friends with benefits, but actually *dating*? I had to say something stupid to distract myself from betraying how much it bothered me that their relationship had worked out that way. "Damn, Alessandro. You must have some serious talent in the bedroom to make Mr. Hetero switch teams permanently."

He grinned wolfishly at me. "If you need any tips, we can talk later."

Callahan got us back on topic. "Wait, so you're *actually* dating? Like, boyfriends in love and not just friends with benefits?"

Lachlan's contented smile told me so much, and it made my heart ache, even as it gave me hope that maybe I'd get lucky someday with Callahan. "Yes, and I couldn't be happier. I was a fool for refusing to see what's been in front of me for so long because I was too scared to take that chance."

"Hint, hint," I added because I was allergic to subtlety.

Callahan ignored my attempts at flirting, as per

usual. "In that case, congrats. You're perfect for each other, so I'm happy for you both." Did I hear a hint of wistfulness in his voice?

It emboldened me to embrace him from behind once more. "And hopefully, you're a little inspired to see where things could go if you gave in to our sexual tension. After all, if it worked out for them, why wouldn't it work out for us?"

"It's never going to happen when I'm a relation-ship guy and the mere thought of being someone's boyfriend gives you hives." Callahan escaped my grasp and jumped out to sit on the edge of the pool with his legs in the water. Shit, I had upset him by pushing too hard. *Again.*

I could have kissed Alessandro when he spoke in my defense. "That's true with everyone else, but some-thing tells me that he'd be different with you."

Oh, that was a guaranteed fact. If I could have Callahan, I wouldn't need anything else to be happy.

"You'll never know if you don't take a chance." Lachlan reached over and tugged Alessandro's flamingo float close enough to hold his hand. He brought it up to his lips to kiss the back of it, which was truly swoon-worthy. "I'm glad I did."

"I'm glad we both did." Alessandro blew him a flirty kiss. "And I look forward to showing you how happy you make me later."

Lachlan launched the schmoopy factor into the

stratosphere with his next response. "And for the rest of our lives."

"One night together and you're already promising forever?" I whistled in an impressed tone. "I've got to hand it to you, Lachlan. When you commit, you *commit*."

"You could learn a thing or two from him," Callahan muttered as he stared glumly at the water.

Well, well, well. *That* certainly wasn't a typical comment from him. I swam over to place myself between his splayed legs as he sat on the pool edge, allowing me to look up into his beautiful emerald eyes. "If you want me to commit to you, all you have to do is say the word."

He scoffed, as if it was the most ridiculous idea in the world. "Yeah, right. You really expect me to believe that Mr. I'm-with-somebody-new-every-night would be with only me?"

Even if I asserted the truth that I'd gladly be with him and only him until the day I died, he'd never accept it. Instead, I opted for a different tactic. "Here's a fun question for you. When was the last time I told you we couldn't hang out or didn't return a text because I was too busy fucking somebody who doesn't matter?"

He opened his mouth but shut it with a consternated expression. That was because we both knew damn well the answer was "Never."

"Can you name one person I've hooked up with lately?"

That earned me an eye roll. "Can *you*? It's not like names are important when all you want is a hot piece of ass."

"Ask yourself this. When I brag about my considerable skills in the bedroom, am I touting my talent to tempt you to experience for yourself? Or am I giving you a laundry list of sexual conquests to impress you?"

Before Callahan answered, Alessandro connected the dots. "Holy *shit*, Baxley."

"What?" Callahan looked at him in confusion.

"*Wow*, you poor bastard," Alessandro said with sympathy. "I guess we were more alike than I thought."

His reaction only confounded Callahan further. "What am I missing here?"

I wasn't about to give him an easy answer. "Think about it. You're smart. You'll figure it out." I just hoped he came to the right conclusion.

Chapter Two

CALLAHAN

EVERY TIME I thought I had Baxley figured out, he found a new way to confuse the hell out of me. My head was still spinning from the revelation that Alessandro and Lachlan were dating when Baxley dropped a riddle bomb on me. It annoyed me that Alessandro understood it while I was still in the dark.

It was true that no matter how busy Baxley was, he always had time for me. He'd drop everything to be with me if I needed him. And there had been plenty of nights where I had dropped by his house late at night on a whim and found him alone. Come to think of it, I had never seen any trace of a visitor in his apartment. But that was probably because he preferred having his sexual encounters at his partner's place, right?

It was true I couldn't name anyone he had been with, but I had witnessed him receiving countless phone numbers from servers after flirting with them throughout the entire meal. Did he really expect me to believe that he wasn't calling them later for a night of no-strings-attached fun?

There was also the third piece of the puzzle to consider. I could think of a million flirty pickup lines he had tried on me, but I couldn't think of a single example where he'd bragged about how many people he had been with. But he wouldn't get skills without considerable practice with others, so something wasn't adding up.

There was more to Alessandro's realization that he and Baxley were more similar than he previously thought. What could that shared reason be?

The answer was *right there*, just beyond my reach. Even as I changed in the bathroom into my regular clothes, I couldn't piece it all together. I was missing some crucial component that would make everything add up.

But it was a problem that could wait for later. I headed back to the living room, only to find Baxley alone on the couch. He appeared to be looking out the wall of windows at the beach beyond the pool deck, but he seemed lost in thought.

Clearing my throat to draw attention to myself, I sat next to him. "I'm assuming they went up for a shower?" Lachlan had a funny quirk about loving his pool and hating the chlorine, so he always showered after we finished. It was only natural that

Alessandro would join him now that they were together.

"Yep. That gives us plenty of time to entertain ourselves while they're gone." He gave me a seductive look that flustered me, which had been happening more often these days.

The longer I was single, the harder it was to say no to his flirtatious offers to take care of me. I was horny, lonely, and he was the person I always turned to for everything. In the dark of night, I kept hearing the insidious whispers from deep within my heart reminding me that a mouth was a mouth and had nothing to do with gender, so why not let him pleasure me with his?

But I couldn't listen, because as soon as I let him do that, I'd feel obligated to jerk him off as a thank-you. We'd end up having sex, and then I'd be stupid and fall in love with him, leaving me destroyed when he moved on to his next conquest. I was a relationship-only guy, and he was allergic to commitment, which was a *terrible* combination. Logically, I understood all that, but it didn't quiet my body's demands that I give in to his teasing.

It was startling to realize I had been rooting for Lachlan and Alessandro to fool around with each other to give me permission to do the same with Baxley. What I hadn't expected was the two of them to drop a bombshell by announcing they were dating. I wasn't at all prepared for them to skip the friends-with-benefits stage and jump headfirst into being boyfriends. That complicated my wants in a way that left me deeply uncomfortable.

Baxley's voice pulled me from my thoughts. "Are you thinking about all the things you want me to do to you right now?"

It was a predictable response, but his questions from before still bugged me. "No, I'm trying to figure out what you were implying in the pool."

"You really can't read between the lines?"

My brain worked overtime to find an answer. However, the only one I could think of was so implausible, it almost wasn't worth mentioning. "I'm obviously missing something, because there's no way in hell you meant what I think you did."

"And what are you so sure I didn't mean?"

"It *almost* sounds like you're suggesting you haven't been with anyone, but that can't be true." I scoffed at the ridiculous notion, although it was the only thing I could come up with that Alessandro would have had in common. He had been *very* salty about being celibate because his heart only wanted Lachlan.

"I'm not suggesting anything. That's exactly what I'm saying."

My jaw dropped in shock before I burst into laughter. "Oh, that's *real* funny. You almost had me for a second, but I know better."

"Do you?" He unlocked his phone and handed it to me. "Notice anything missing?"

I flipped through his apps, then backtracked through them because I had to be mistaken. How was it possible that there wasn't a single dating app on his phone? He was too busy to find that many partners without something like that speeding up the process. Just to be sure, I opened the app store to see if he had deleted them to make me think something that wasn't true. But none of them had ever been downloaded, which floored me. I stared up at him in disbelief. "I don't understand."

"If you can't figure it out with that kind of hint, it's because you don't want to acknowledge the truth."

It took me a few stammered attempts at words before I could collect myself enough to respond. "But it doesn't make sense! Are you seriously sitting there and telling me you've been lying this whole time about your *very* active sex life?"

"*I* haven't been lying. *You* have been making assumptions about me I never corrected. That's different."

"How the hell is that possible?" There was no way that was true, right? Because if it *was*, it would make me a *huge* asshole.

"You equated me flirting with you about how well I could take care of you with me fucking everyone as practice."

I grasped at straws as I tried to prove him wrong. "But—but you get phone numbers from people *all the time*."

He shrugged like it wasn't a big deal. "That doesn't mean I contact them."

"Then what the hell do you do with them?"

"I throw them away. Check my text messages. You'll see I'm telling the truth."

It couldn't be true. But I pulled up his texts like he told me. Instead of the long list of random hookup hotties I had expected to see, there weren't any anonymous numbers or names I didn't recognize. The only recent contacts were his family, me, Alessandro, Lachlan, our group chat, and his boss.

"I don't understand. What's going on?" I looked at him, expecting him to burst into laughter that it was all one big joke and he got me good. But he was so serious, I knew he was being truthful. He might have been a huge flirt, but he wasn't a liar. "Please make this make sense. Because I'm *this* close to crawling into a hole and dying of shame right now. I'm begging you, please tell me I'm not that much of an asshole and a terrible friend."

"You're neither of those things," he said in a gentle voice as he took his phone back and pocketed it. "I think you were so scared of feeling something about me that you told yourself what you needed to hear to make me off-limits."

His answer hit me hard in the weak spot of the shadows of my heart that had always been a little *too* drawn to Baxley. Because he was absolutely right. He had to be the antithesis of everything I stood for, because if I knew he was the kind of guy who wanted to be in a serious, committed relationship with me, then I'd never be able to resist my feelings that had been growing louder and louder every passing night that encouraged me to give in to his teasing.

"Why would you let me do that?" I demanded in anguish. "Why the fuck didn't you correct me?"

"Would you have believed me if I told you a playful flirt like me hasn't fucked someone in three years?" He snorted in amusement. "Hell, *I* barely believe it, and I *know* I've been living like a monk."

"Three years?" I swallowed hard as the info made my head spin. "But we met three years ago."

"Yep."

"That's all you have to say? *Yep?*" I spluttered in my confusion. "*Why?* Why has it been *three years* since you've been with someone?"

"For the same reason you're always telling me: you're a relationship-only guy. You'd never be with me if I was fucking around for real. Plus, none of them were you, so there was no point."

A strangled keen escaped me at what he was saying. "Are you telling me you haven't had a partner in three years because of *me*, even though I've been the world's biggest asshole accusing you of hooking up with anyone hot enough?"

"Surprise."

I was appalled with myself and completely floored by the information. "How do you not hate me? I've talked *so much shit* about you being with other people, but you've always just laughed it off."

"One, I could never hate you. Two, part of our dynamic involves being ballbusters and making fun of each other. Three, every time you complained about me being with other men, I got the chance to tell myself that maybe you were protesting because you were jealous and secretly developing feelings for me." He gave me his trademark lopsided grin that made my heart do funny things I had been trying so hard to ignore. "You should take it as a compliment that I find flirting with you more satisfying than sex with a random stranger."

The nonstop revelations left me reeling. I struggled not to lose myself in the bombarding rush of emotions he stirred up within me. "But *why?*"

He looked at me with a bemused expression. "You really don't know why?"

I shook my head because I didn't trust myself to talk. When he reached over and cupped his hand against my flushed cheek with heartbreaking tenderness, I stopped breathing.

"Because it's apparently obvious to everyone but you that I've been stupid in love with you since we met."

Baxley loved me? Mr. Shameless Flirt had secretly been devoted to me for *three years?* Because he *loved* me? I wanted to deny it and insist he stop bullshitting me. But it was impossible when I knew deep down that he was telling me the truth. The gentle brush of his thumb against my cheekbone made my heart stutter in my chest and further emphasized his sincerity. Somehow, the man I thought had been allergic to commitment had been loyal to me for three damn years, even when I assumed the worst of him? How was that possible?

As overwhelmed as I was, my brain took a back seat as I reacted purely on instinct. I didn't let myself overthink as I straddled myself over his lap and kissed him with my jumbled mess of chaotic feelings toward him that had built up inside of me.

The floodgates opened as he held the back of my neck and tugged me closer. I got a taste of his passion, *and I fucking loved it.*

Chapter Three

BAXLEY

MY WORLD EXPLODED into starlight and sunfire when Callahan straddled my lap and kissed me like he had been dying to do it forever. I tugged him closer as I claimed his lips for mine, the way I had been dreaming about doing since the night I first met him. It was the best kind of heaven to have him on top of me as I ravaged his mouth with the passionate desire I had been holding back for three *long* years. It got even better when he entangled his fingers in my hair as he slaked his thirst with kiss after kiss.

I boldly slipped my hands under his tank to touch his tempting bare skin. It earned me a delicious gasp as he rocked against me while still trying to kiss me senseless. I continued caressing him, heightening the pleasure for both of us. To my great delight, his shorts did a terrible job of hiding his growing arousal that pressed against me. I was ready to carry him upstairs to one of Lachlan's unused bedrooms, but I didn't want to stop kissing him long enough to do it.

For once in my life, I had the good sense to keep my smart-ass comments to myself and not ruin the moment by saying something flippant. Callahan stared at me with a stunned expression as his fingers reflexively stroked my hair that he hadn't let go of yet. He endeared himself to me further when he murmured with awe, "*Wow.*"

"Wow, indeed." I wrapped my arms around his waist as I held him closer. When he didn't reject me, I rejoiced.

He stayed silent for a bit as he tried to sort through his reaction. "That was...I don't have the words for it."

"I'm taking it as a good sign that you're still in my lap instead of running away."

Callahan blushed as he shifted against me. "I'm definitely not running away after that."

I might have gotten a taste of what I wanted most, but I couldn't resist teasing him a little. "Not with that hard-on you're not." I burst into laughter at his outraged reaction.

He shoved at my shoulder with a scowl. "Hey, that's *your* fault! I haven't been kissed like that since— well, since *ever*. And if that's you when you're three years out of practice? I don't stand a chance against you."

"I stayed in practice by dreaming about how good

it would be to kiss you."

His eyebrows arched up. "*Just* kiss me?"

"If you'd like a demonstration of what else I've fantasized about, I'd be more than happy to indulge your curiosity. Lachlan has so many rooms in this place, I bet I could make you come at least twice before he found us."

It was cute how scandalized he was by my suggestion. "We can't do that!"

"Why not? He offered to let us use one of his spare rooms yesterday. I can't imagine he would object today. In the unlikely event he did, I'm pretty sure Alessandro could talk him into allowing it." Callahan's flustered reaction made me want to play with him even more. "Or I could lay you out on this coffee table and suck your dick right here while we wait for them to finish upstairs."

His pale eyelashes fluttered at the suggestion as he rocked his hardness against me with a pained noise. "Stop tempting me with stuff I shouldn't want!"

"Is it the offer for a blow job or the location that you're objecting to? Because if it's only the latter, I will carry you out of here caveman-style back to my place where I can pleasure you without fear of interruptions."

"But we're supposed to hang out with Alessandro and Lachlan today."

"They'll forgive us for bailing on them under the circumstances." I cupped his arousal, earning a hiss of shock. "But if you'd rather cool off in the pool instead of letting me take care of you, that's your call."

He made my heart sing when he decided without hesitation. "Your place it is." Sweeping him up in my arms, I delighted in his shocked giggle as he clung to me. "Wait, what about our stuff?"

"Lachlan's more than capable of guarding our laundry until we come back. We have much more pressing matters to attend to."

Callahan's light laughter filled my heart with sunshine and happiness as I carried him out to my car. It took three years to reach that point in our relationship, but it was well worth the wait. I looked forward to the challenge of making up for lost time once we returned to my apartment.

CALLAHAN'S earlier confidence boost seemed to fade into uncertainty as he stood in my bedroom with a self-conscious expression. I set about reassuring him with a gentle kiss, letting my lips whisper to him that I was going to treasure every inch of him. He melted against me with a soft sigh, fisting my shirt in his hands as he submitted to me. Once he relaxed, I reached down to remove his white tank.

To my surprise, he stopped me with a nervous look. "We're not doing anything, uh, *penetrative*, are we? Because I don't think I'm there yet."

I didn't take offense to his concerns. As someone who had always identified as a straight man, his uneasiness with the prospect was understandable. I had plenty of time to ease him into that later. "You have my word. All I want to do is cover you in kisses before I give you the best blow job of your life."

Accepting my promise, he let me remove his tank and cast it aside. I then put on a show of stripping off my shirt, shorts, and underwear, letting my erection spring free. It was only fair to give him a chance to back out before I bared him completely.

It was precious how he blushed at the sight of my arousal. "Now that I know you haven't been with anyone for three years, your raging horniness makes a *lot* more sense."

I reached down to stroke my length as I held his gaze. "This has everything to do with finally being blessed enough to have the chance to prove to you I'm not all talk."

He blinked at me several times with a dazed look.

Not wanting to overwhelm him with too much too soon, I stopped touching myself. "Are you having second thoughts?"

He shook his head, making me breathe a sigh of relief. "No, I'm confused."

"About what?"

He bit his lower lip. "You're going to laugh at me."

"In theory, that should reassure you since that's

the norm." My words earned me the chuckle I knew they would. "But if it'll make you feel better, I promise I'll try *really* hard not to."

He took a deep breath as he squared his shoulders with resolve. "I might have had a few inappropriate late-night thoughts wondering what it would be like if I ever said yes to your offers to suck my dick."

What a delightful kernel of knowledge *that* was. Rather than thanking him for giving me something new to fantasize about, I nodded to show I was listening, and he should continue.

"We're always clothed when you tugged my pants down when I reached the point where I couldn't take the teasing anymore." He looked away in embarrassment. "I never pictured either of us being completely naked."

"Would it make you more comfortable if I put my clothes back on?"

"No, but I feel like I'm supposed to have a squeamish straight-guy reaction to seeing you jerking off, but, um…"

I was *dying* to know how that sentence ended. "You can tell me."

He looked up at the ceiling with a pained expression. "I can't say it. It's going to make me sound *so* self-centered."

"That's fine. It's hot when your ego comes out to play a little." Grinning at him, I tried to convince him some more. "It should be fairly obvious by this point that I love it when you're a bit of a bastard. Lay it on me."

It took him a few moments to build up the courage to confess. "Instead of being grossed out watching you touching yourself, it's kind of…um, well, it's sort of sexy seeing how turned on you are because of me. I don't know what to do with that reaction."

"You've got plenty of time to overanalyze it later. All that matters right now is you're into this."

He drew a shuddering breath. "*Way* more than I was expecting."

I closed the distance between us to give him a searing kiss to refocus his attention on what was happening. He whimpered into it as I let my hands wander over his bare skin. I slowly worked down to his shorts, unbuttoning them and sending them to the floor.

I stopped shy of my goal, even as I took a moment to appreciate the bulge straining in his navy briefs. "Do you want me to keep going?"

"Dear god, *please*."

I added making him beg to the list of things I looked forward to doing later. Taking my time, I lowered his underwear until he was gloriously bared before me. His cock stood up at full attention, beckoning me to attend to it. As much as I wanted to fall to my knees and gratefully accept the gift he was bestowing upon me, I intended to worship the rest of him first.

Chapter Four

CALLAHAN

NONE of the fantasies I had reluctantly entertained about Baxley sucking my dick had involved being naked or near a bed. I was completely out of my depths when he gestured for me to make myself comfortable on his plush duvet cover. But he didn't give me long to dwell before he covered my body with his and gave me an insistent kiss I surrendered to. His passion burned away any reservations I had left as he dominated my desires. Even his erection brushing against me was turning me on.

Everything felt so good that I questioned why the hell I'd resisted his playful flirtations for three damn years. That question echoed through me as he started trailing kisses down my jaw and neck. I shivered as he pressed his lips against the freckles on one of my shoulders. But it also made me realize something. "Wait, why are you doing that?"

"Because I fucking *love* your cute little freckles." He continued kissing a path amongst them.

I had always been self-conscious about them, so it stunned me to hear. "Really?"

"They're one of my favorite parts of the summer." He said it with so much sincerity, it took me aback. "Seeing them peeking out from under your tank makes it damn near impossible to keep my hands to myself."

His confession filled me with a warm glow before I remembered my point. "But why are you doing that when I'm gross right now?"

He stopped to look up at me in confusion. "Gross how?"

"Unless you have a kink for sunscreen and chlorine, shouldn't I at least take a shower first?"

"You taste like summer and all my dreams coming true." He continued kissing down my chest, making my breathing hitch when he reached one of my nipples.

It was the most romantic thing anyone had ever said to me. However, it threw me for a loop that it was *Baxley* using such a smooth line on me. "Wow, if you're saying that, you must *really* have it bad for me."

"Since the very first moment I saw you, before you had even said a word to me."

His claim stunned me. "What are you talking about?"

"When I went to Lachlan's housewarming party, I

watched you talking to Alessandro before he introduced us. I fell for your cute little giggle, the way your eyes crinkle when you laugh, and your ornery grin when you make a joke. Once I spoke with you, I knew you were it for me."

It was difficult to focus on the conversation when he playfully tugged on my nipple with his teeth. The gesture made me achingly hard, but I did my best to stay on track. "You can't be serious!"

"Why not?"

"Because you're a self-admitted playboy!"

He teased my other nipple into a taut peak with his fingers. "Self-admitted *former* playboy. Nobody has ever captured my attention like you, so I retired from that. You're the only one who was worth the effort of chasing."

I had never forgotten his opening introduction. "Is *that* why the first thing you said to me was 'You look like my happily ever after' when Alessandro introduced us?"

"Yep, that wasn't a cheesy pickup line. It was me speaking the absolute truth."

My jaw dropped in shock as I tried to process the implications. "But if that's how you felt, why did you hide it behind jokes for so long?"

"As you'll recall, you were dating Julissa at the time." He began kissing lower, which rocketed my heart into my throat. "I'm a lot of things, but a home wrecker isn't one of them."

"Not intentionally, at least."

He paused as he looked up at me with a puzzled expression. "What do you mean?"

"Never mind. Forget I said that." It was so hard to have an active filter when Baxley's lips and fingertips obliterated everything in my brain.

He stroked my hip in comfort. "I'd appreciate if you told me."

Steeling myself, I confessed something I had never admitted to him before. "I left her because of you."

His eyebrows furrowed in confusion. "I thought you broke up with her because she was too clinging and overbearing?"

"Those were the main reasons. But the incident that triggered the breakup was her picking a fight with me about spending too much time with you instead of being with her." The memory made me cringe. "She told me I had to choose between her and you. Hanging out with you was way more fun than being around her, so I chose you. But I couldn't tell you back then because we had only known each other a few weeks at that point. I didn't want to give you the wrong impression. And then Mireya added to that, so…"

"You lost me again."

I had to crack a joke to lighten the mood. "Probably because too much blood is flowing to your dick for your brain to keep up."

"Yeah, probably," he agreed with a laugh. "But

what do you mean about Mireya? You only dated her for a couple of weeks."

"That's because on our third date, she informed me that she was uncomfortable with how close I was to you. She said if I wanted to be with her, I had to quit seeing you so much. I replied I wouldn't do that because you meant more to me than she did, and that was the end of that. After two ex-girlfriends who tried to make me choose between them and you, I decided it was easier to be single for a while. I'd always pick you over them, anyway."

Baxley moved up to give me an ardent kiss that I moaned into as I laced my fingers in his dark hair. I lost myself in his passion, making me wonder how the fuck I had misinterpreted my own motivations for picking him over my girlfriends. But I didn't have two brain cells left to rub together, so I quit worrying about it.

Baxley rewarded me further by moving down to position himself between my legs. He gave my cock a few teasing strokes that sent electricity zinging through my body. "Fuck, and I thought I was excited to suck your dick before. Knowing you chose me over two ex-girlfriends? I'm going to make sure you come so hard, you'll see stars."

Whatever smart-ass retort I tried to come up with disappeared when he began kissing along my length until he reached the tip. He put on a show of teasing it before he let me slide into his mouth. It hadn't been three years of celibacy for me, but after months of being single, the wet warmth was a total shock to my system.

He worked up to a satisfying rhythm as he alternated between sucking and stroking my length. By the time he deep-throated me, I trembled from the overwhelming pleasure that exceeded the hype he had been tempting me with for years. I grounded myself by lacing my fingers through his hair. As he made my toes curl from the ecstasy of satiating my sexual curiosity, I stroked the back of his head.

All my muscles tensed in anticipation of the promising tingle threatening to overtake me. I hated coming to a premature end, but it felt too good after so many months of only having my right hand to gratify myself. "Bax, I'm so close!"

He took me all the way in with a rumble in his throat that made me come with a gasp. Everything went hazy as I watched him swallow my release and pull back to wipe the corner of his mouth with his thumb.

Since I didn't have any brain left, I said the first thought that popped into my head. "Holy fuck, how are you actually *better* than what you boasted about being capable of doing?"

He moved to stretch out beside me. "Maybe now you'll believe I'm good enough to follow through on my other promises to rock your world, if you'd only give me the chance."

"After that, you can do damn near anything you want to me once I have the energy. That was *incredible*." As amazing as I felt, it took a bit before I remembered that while I had gotten off, he was still rock-hard and patiently waiting.

It drove me to boldness as I reached over and wrapped my hand around his erection. I relished his shocked gasp, finding unexpected pleasure in his reaction. It gave me the courage to keep going until I made him come.

Chapter Five

BAXLEY

OUT OF ALL THE reactions I had expected, having Callahan jerk me off hadn't been one of them. But he took hold of my dick with the confidence of a man who did it all the time. His grip was firm and sure as he worked my length with an ornery gleam in his eyes.

A soft sigh escaped from me when he added some flair to his pumps. "Mmm, just like that." It took a monumental effort not to call him "Baby" like I did in all my fantasies.

"It's funny. I assumed I'd feel like I had to do this out of obligation as a thank-you." His eyes were bright with interest as he looked me over. "But it's fucking hot having you at my mercy."

I reached up to caress his cheek as I grinned at him. "Does the thought of me being submissive please you?"

He made an indecisive noise. "No, I don't want you *completely* submissive, because that's too boring. But it's really doing it for me to have Mr. Big Talk surrender to me for the sake of pleasure."

"Didn't we agree I'm not all talk?" Teasing him was too much fun. "Or are you requesting another demonstration of my skills later?"

His delighted giggle loosened my residual fear that maybe I had pushed him too fast in exploring a new side of his sexuality. "I'm going to need some time to recover first."

My next retort disappeared when he moved in closer to suck on my earlobe, then tug on it with his teeth.

It set me off. I moaned his name as I came hard enough that my cum almost made it as far as my chest. He looked so smug I couldn't resist teasing him. "Are you pleased with yourself?"

"Inordinately," he admitted with a broad grin. "I'm verging on a full-blown power trip at this point. *I* made *you* come."

He deserved a little more ego stroking after the orgasm he gave me. "More times than you can count if we include all the occasions I've gotten myself off to fantasies of being with you."

"How did you suddenly flip the switch in my brain to make me think that's sexy instead of causing me to roll my eyes?" He shook his head in disbelief. "I don't understand."

"From the sounds of it, it's not so sudden. Even you have to admit you've been more receptive to my flirting recently."

"I thought it was out of desperation because it's been months since I've been with a woman." He shrugged with a frown. "But it seems there's been more going on in the back of my mind than I was aware of."

I reached over to my nightstand to grab a tissue for me and another for Callahan to clean up my mess. "Does it bother you?"

"I don't think so?" He sounded uncertain. "I feel like it should, but this felt so good I don't actually care?"

"If you want to skip the overthinking part and just have fun enjoying each other, you won't get any complaints from me." I said a secret prayer he went with that option. It would devastate me if he had second thoughts and decided he didn't want to be with me after.

"Like, part of me really wants to kiss you right now, but the rest of me is grossed out because I came in your mouth." He scrunched up his nose in adorable disgust. "But I felt the same way about kissing my girlfriends after they gave me a blow job, so that might just be a me thing."

It was such a cute protest I couldn't get offended by it. "It's definitely a you thing, but that's fine. There's no judgment here."

"But what if I can never bring myself to give you one and swallow?"

"That's not a deal breaker for me. But we can talk about it later." I pressed a kiss to his forehead. "Let's get lunch."

His expression grew apprehensive. "Does that mean things are back to normal?"

"Not in the sense of we did that, and now we act like nothing happened." I tried to lighten the mood. "You should understand me well enough to know I have no intention of stopping there after I've enjoyed a taste of you. I'm nothing if not persistent."

"Try relentless." Relief washed over him. "Wow, it says something about me that hearing that makes me feel better, doesn't it?"

"Then let me be explicitly clear: I'm not interested in enjoying some meaningless sex with you and breaking your heart."

He fought back a pleased smile. "What are you interested in instead?"

"I want to enjoy *very* meaningful sex with you and give you my heart, if you want it."

All the shadows fled from his eyes as he laughed. "Well, in that case, I definitely want it." He propped himself up and gave me a chaste kiss on the lips, which I knew was huge for him.

I didn't push for more than he was willing to give. "Wanting to get lunch has everything to do with caring about your well-being and selfishly making sure you have the energy to keep up with me later."

"Brush your teeth, and let's go. I'm suddenly *ravenous*."

He didn't need to tell me twice. Knowing we were on the same page was all I needed to keep me going. Before the end of the night, I would make him mine.

Chapter Six

CALLAHAN

AS WE FINISHED LUNCH, my nerves crept up on me about what would happen later. Like he always did, Baxley picked up on my anxiety. "What are you overthinking, Callahan?"

I fidgeted before I fessed up to the truth. "I'm wondering if being…*intimidated* by anal sex makes me homophobic?"

For once, he didn't laugh at me. "It doesn't. With something that's so far out of your normal comfort zone and range of experience, it makes logical sense that you find the prospect a little overwhelming. No one is saying that has to happen today or any other day."

His answer made me feel marginally better about my trepidation. "Don't get me wrong. I'm curious, but you also know I'm a total wuss about pain."

He rested his elbows on the table as he held his

chin in the palm of his hand. "What I find interesting is you *always* assume that you'll be on the receiving end of pleasure with me."

I blushed hard. "Well, yeah. I'm not gay, but I know you're a top."

"What makes you say that?"

"Uh, everything about you?" I laughed nervously as I shifted in my chair. "You're cocksure, you've aggressively pursued me, and you're always talking about the pleasures you want to give me. Of *course* I'd assume you're a top because of that."

He hummed with interest. "You've never once considered that I might enjoy being topped by you?"

"Why would you?" I snorted at the absurd prospect.

"Because being with you under any circumstances or position would be worth it to me."

His response flustered me. "Are you saying you'll let me take you?"

"That's exactly what I'm saying." His blue eyes were bright with interest. "As hard or gentle as you like."

I may have had some reservations, but my dick was *definitely* into the idea. "You'd really let me fuck you?"

"Hell, I'd let you do me on this table in front of this whole restaurant at this point." He laughed at my stunned expression. "You're severely underestimating how much I want to be with you."

"Is that the only reason you'd let me do that?" The thought made me frown. "Because you think that's the only way you can be with me?"

The playfulness disappeared from his expression as he turned serious. "No, what I'm saying is that anything we do is going to be amazing. Who's on top or the bottom is irrelevant. Sexual positions don't define our roles in a relationship. We're equals, no matter what we do in bed, on a table, in the shower, against a wall, in my car, on the—"

I held up my hand to stop him, because his list of places we could have sex was getting me spun up inside. "Point taken. But be honest with me: if I said I would *never* bottom, wouldn't that be a problem for you?"

"Nope."

My jaw dropped at how easily he replied. "How can you say that? You're *such* a top."

"True, but my sincere answer is that I respect you enough to never make you do anything you're uncomfortable with. I'd rather be on the bottom for the rest of my life than never being with you at all."

It was an unexpectedly sweet response that caught me off guard. "And your insincere answer?"

"You can say you won't do it, but we both know that's a braggadocios lie," he said with the utmost certainty.

"*Braggadocios*? Really?"

"Yes, because your curiosity will inevitably get the

better of you when you see how much I enjoy it. It's going to drive you nuts until you try it yourself to see if it's possible to derive that much pleasure from anal sex." His confidence annoyed me—especially because I knew he was right. My curiosity always got the best of me in the end. "You'll stew about it while you try to talk yourself out of it until it boils over and you demand that I fuck you. I'll enjoy proving to you yet again that I've got the talent to back up my big promises."

It was easy to imagine myself under him, arching up as he thrust into me. My fear told me it would hurt, but my trust in Baxley swore it would be amazing. That was something I'd have to figure out later. First, I was going to learn what pleasures his body could offer me.

BACK IN BAXLEY'S BEDROOM, I was ready to find out if having sex with a man was anywhere as pleasurable as being with a woman. By the time I had him pinned on the bed under me, my head was already spinning from the rush of lust. The way his hands wandered over my body as we kissed sent electric shivers racing down my spine. They were rougher than my ex-girlfriends and lacked their nails, but somehow that made it more exciting for me.

I surprised both of us when I shifted down and

started exploring his body with more confidence than I felt. While he didn't have the large swell of breasts like my girlfriends, I still toyed with his nipples. They pebbled under my attention, earning me breathy sighs as I continued teasing them with my tongue and tugged on them to see if he liked that. If the insistent pressing of his hard-on against my belly was any indication, he was *definitely* into it. Shockingly, so was I.

As I moved down, I encountered his faint happy trail. Shifting into a more comfortable position, I followed the path down to his well-manscaped pubes. His erection jutted out, flushed and demanding attention. I gave it a few strokes, then smeared the bead of precum over the top. It was a mystery to me why my "Eww, gross" reaction never seemed to kick in. "How is it that touching your dick feels completely strange and utterly normal all at the same time?"

"Because I've spent three years trying to talk you into this moment."

I shifted my attention to his scrotum. I had never seen anyone else's up close, so I took my time exploring and fondling it as I tried to figure out my reaction. "My brain keeps telling me this should weird me out."

"My balls specifically, or touching me sexually in general?"

I cracked up at his ridiculous question. "I don't know. Maybe both? You don't think it's strange?"

"The only odd thing is that this is finally

happening for real and not just in my imagination." He moved his leg to give me more room to explore.

My heart skipped a beat as I let my fingers trail down over his perineum to his entrance. "This is what you really want?"

"More than anything," he groaned with need. "The real question is, would you prefer to do it yourself or watch me do it?"

Maybe it was all the blood rushing south or my inexperience with being with a man, but I didn't follow. "Do what?"

The corner of his lips quirked up in a smirk. "Allow me to demonstrate." He stretched out to grab a bottle of lube from his nightstand, then gestured for me to move into a better position.

I watched in fascination as Baxley inserted slicked fingers into himself. My brain short-circuited while I watched him fuck himself. He put on a hell of a show as he tugged on his dick with his free hand, whimpering my name.

It made my lust burn like wildfire as I imagined him doing that while thinking about me whenever he was alone. There was something unspeakably arousing about him pleasuring himself and wishing it were me instead. It gave me the push I needed to get me over the last of my fears. I swallowed hard, and my voice trembled as I asked, "When is it my turn?"

Baxley withdrew his fingers from within him with an obscene squelch of the lube, then wiped them clean on a tissue off his nightstand. "As soon as you figure out how you want me."

I didn't have enough blood left to run both my brain and fuel my hard-on. "What do you mean, how do I want you?"

"Do you want me like this? Or would you prefer me on my hands and knees as you take me from behind?"

I wrinkled my nose in distaste. "Definitely not the last one."

One of his dark eyebrows arched up. "What's wrong with that?"

"I don't know. It seems impersonal and disrespectful?" I shrugged because I knew it was a weird reaction.

"How so?"

His question made me wish I had kept my damn mouth shut. "Because it makes me feel like I'm using my partner only for their hole. They could be anyone if I can't see their face and know it's them."

His smile broadened into a pleased grin. "Is that your way of saying you want to see me?"

"I'd rather see your face than the back of your head, yeah," I mumbled in embarrassment.

He sat up and guided me to kiss him, cradling my cheeks in his hands. "You're too cute for words."

"Why does that make me cute?"

"Because it means you want to be with *me*, rather

than picturing a woman as you fuck me. That makes you extra adorable in my book."

His choice of phrase made me scowl. "Could we not call it fucking? It just sounds so…"

His happiness caused my heart to somersault in my chest. "Would you prefer if I said making love?"

"No, that's too embarrassing! Not to mention it puts *way* too much pressure on me to perform."

He chuckled at my reaction. "Fine. It makes me feel good to know that you'd rather be intimate with me than some random woman. Is that better?"

"Marginally." I didn't have the brainpower to keep arguing semantics, so I let the issue go. "Condoms?"

"Ah, that is the one flaw in my grand master plan. I don't have any because I haven't been with anyone in so long. Plus, I wasn't quite *that* optimistic about my odds of getting you to agree to be with me."

I couldn't hold back my pout. "Wait, so we went through all that buildup for nothing?"

"Are you worried about getting me pregnant?" His cheeky grin made me burst into laughter. "Sorry to break it to you, but that's not how it works between two guys. If you're worried about the other parts, I've been living like a monk for years. I've been tested, so I'm not putting you at risk of anything other than having a great time."

"Same here, but is it really okay?" I bit my lower lip as I looked at him uncertainly. "It'll be so messy."

"Let me worry about doing the laundry afterward.

Focus on feeling good right now." He reached down and stroked my erection a few times to coat it with lube. "Don't worry about hurting me. Just because I haven't been with a man in years doesn't mean I'm out of practice."

A fuse blew in my brain at the innuendo his smirk implied. "Wait, you use *dildos* on yourself?"

He couldn't hold back his laughter. "Why are you so scandalized by that?"

"Because you're a *top*! Tops don't put things in their own ass! They put their dicks in *other people's* asses."

"We need to work on fixing your assumptions later." Amusement radiated off him in waves. "I told you before: I enjoy changing things up, which means yes, I love being penetrated when I'm in the mood. Since I couldn't have you, I had to make do with silicone in the meantime."

A mental picture of Baxley fucking himself with a dildo as he moaned my name made me shiver with an unexpected flare of arousal.

He looked infuriatingly smug. "Like that, don't you?"

"A little too much," I muttered, confused by my own reaction.

He stretched out on the bed once more, spreading his legs wide as he reached down and ran his fingers over his entrance. "Come find out what you've been missing."

My body seemed to move on autopilot as I lined myself up. It felt like being a virgin all over again as my nerves preyed on my uncertainty.

As if sensing the direction my thoughts had taken, he reassured me. "The mechanics aren't any different. You'll be fine once you let go and have fun."

Taking him at his word, I guided myself into him. Having always used condoms with my ex-girlfriends, I was unprepared for the difference not having one made. The slick heat embracing me was like nothing I had experienced before. I pushed in deeper when I realized I wasn't hurting him. "What the hell? How does it already feel *this* good? We haven't done anything yet!"

He chuckled as he tightened around me, making me thrust into the sensation. "You're welcome to start."

I couldn't have stopped myself, even if I had wanted to. While I started out cautiously, that didn't last long in the face of pleasure. An explosion of sexual ecstasy detonated inside me as I picked up speed. All thoughts of strangeness fled as I lost myself in the exquisite experience of being buried in my best friend. It got even better when he reached up to loop his arms over my neck. He laced his fingers through my hair in a gentle caress as we moved together. We kissed with passionate need, breaking apart when the shift in angles made Baxley cry out.

It was a sound I needed to hear again, so I redoubled my efforts. Hitching one of his legs around my waist, I gripped his ass to help guide our movements. How had I never noticed what a nice one he had before now?

Considering how dirty he talked normally, I hadn't expected him to be so sensuous. His soft moans and sighs sounding like an erotic symphony that I was ready to buy season tickets to enjoy on a long-term basis.

It was an unexpected reaction, especially after my last girlfriend. She had been noisy as hell in the bedroom, making me cringe when she started making high-pitched, loud squawks. It always sounded overly forced, like she was trying to prove to anyone within a five-block radius that she was *really* enjoying herself. Even if I barely touched her, she was nearly screaming as if she was shooting amateur porn for hidden cameras. Sometimes I had wished I could get away with faking a kink where I got off on her being gagged to smother her incessant screeches and babbling.

But Baxley's deep, masculine sounds of enjoyment fueled my raging fire of desire. Not only that, but I wanted him to make more noise. Hearing him cry out my name made me shudder every time from the intense pleasure it sent coursing through my veins. I loved how he held on to me like I was the only thing keeping him from being swept away by the tidal wave of ecstasy descending on us.

Although I had believed his earnest confession earlier, it wasn't until that moment that I fully understood how he felt about me. More than that, it also brought me to the startling realization that I had more feelings for him than I had let myself be aware of. It was an undeniable fact that I wanted more of Baxley. Thankfully, I knew he'd never deny me anything.

Chapter Seven

BAXLEY

IT WAS interesting discovering my vivid imagination had done a shitty job of predicting just how incredible being intimate with Callahan was. He looked down at me with awed wonder as he brought me to new heights with his gentleness. It felt like my heart would explode from my overwhelming love for him as we moved together as one. He was everything I had ever wanted and so much more.

As I raced to the precipice of my climax, I reached down and started jerking myself off. I didn't want things to be over, but I also was dying to come after too much teasing.

"Oh, *Bax*!" Hearing him calling out my name was the push that took me right to the edge.

Two more strokes were all I needed to shoot my load all over my stomach as I cried out. "Callahan!"

I hadn't expected it to trigger his orgasm. He pushed in deep, then came inside me with a moan. It felt even better than normal because of the lack of condom, and it was the love of my life claiming me as his.

Guiding him closer, I gave him a kiss that I hoped conveyed all my affection and adoration for him. I needed him more than he understood, and I could only hope and pray that someday he would come to want me, too.

The sadness I experienced when he withdrew disappeared into delight as he collapsed on top of me with a satisfied and protracted moan. I wrapped my arms around him and held him tight, pressing a kiss to his forehead. It amazed me he did that, considering how fastidious he was, and my stomach was far from clean thanks to our activities.

We remained in a companionable silence, adrift in the afterglow. I assumed he had fallen asleep until he breathed in an awed voice, "Damn, and I thought what we did before felt good. That was…*wow*."

I chuckled at his amazement. "That seems like a bit of an understatement, actually."

"At best, I had hoped it would feel like normal sex. I wasn't prepared for it to be *that* spectacular. Is it always *that* amazing?"

"Only when you're with someone you love." It was a sappy answer but also a true one.

He was silent for a long pause before he said words that made my heart stutter in my chest. "Then maybe I love you, too."

I could only whisper his name in shock. Out of all the potential reactions he could have to us being intimate, that hadn't been one I expected.

He stunned me further when he added, "Maybe I always have, and I just didn't realize it before."

I hugged him tighter. Could I really be *that* lucky?

He continued thinking out loud. "It might be the unbelievably satisfying orgasm talking, but it makes a lot of sense. It would explain my inappropriate jealousy whenever I thought about you hooking up with other people. There's also the selfish way I'd try to monopolize your evenings so you couldn't go out on dates with someone else. I wanted you all to myself, but I assumed it was just as a friend. Looks like I was dead-ass wrong about the source of all my feelings about you."

His realization made my heart soar. "I'm yours, whether you want me or not. That's as true now as it has been for the past three years."

I could feel the heated flush of his cheek on my shoulder. "It's pretty safe to say I want you, too. I need more of you, more of that, more of everything."

They were words I had always hoped to hear. "Then I'm yours."

"Not to ruin the moment—because I know I

should kiss you after saying something that romantic —but I still don't have the energy to move after such an intense orgasm."

I laughed hard at how precious he was. "That's fine. Being blissed-out is an acceptable excuse. I'll accept a rain check under the circumstances."

He tilted his head to press a kiss to my shoulder. "I'm sorry I made us wait so many years for this. I don't know what else I can say other than I'm a dumbass who should be ashamed of himself."

I caressed his hair to soothe away his concerns. "There's no reason to feel bad. The chase made it even more satisfying when you finally gave in to me."

"Does that mean you won't chase me anymore now that you have me?"

I laughed at his mistaken assumption. "If you think for one minute that I'm ever going to stop pursuing you, then you don't know me that well."

"So you're saying I should expect the same teasing, only we get sexual satisfaction out of it once we're alone?"

His question made me grin. "Provided I can wait that long. I'm sure Lachlan and Alessandro wouldn't mind us engaging in a little foreplay while they're busy enjoying themselves."

"We are *not* doing this in front of them!" He sounded aghast in his protest, which only caused me to laugh harder.

"Fine. To preserve your modesty, we'll compromise by claiming a bedroom in his beach house for ourselves to escape to when we can't keep our hands to ourselves."

He scoffed at my idea. "We're *not* doing that."

"I'll remind you about this conversation the next time I give you a hard-on while all four of us are in the pool together."

Callahan hid his face against my shoulder with a pained groan. "Please don't. I'll die of embarrassment."

"Hey, that's between you and your dick," I teased him. "I can't help it if you find me so sexy that it wants to come out to play."

"Do you have any idea how annoying it is that I want to scoff about you and sexy not belonging in the same sentence, but I can't do that now?" He huffed in irritation. "You play dirty."

"Yeah, because it's more fun." I let my hand sneak down to cop a feel of his ass. His squeak of surprise made me laugh. "You'll see."

"Right now, I'm more concerned about how dirty your sheets are because of us," he grumbled. "Not to mention the mess I'm lying in."

I grinned as his clean-bean gene kicked in. "There's no point in changing them when I'm not done with you yet."

He groaned in protest. "Sorry, but I'm down for the count."

"Sure, at the moment. Later is a different story."

His incredulous giggle made me smile, even though I was serious. Now that I knew he wanted me, there was no holding back.

Chapter Eight

CALLAHAN

AS WE FINISHED EATING our takeout dinner at Baxley's apartment, my trademark bluntness got the better of my mouth. "What are your intentions after we're done?"

"My intentions to do what?" Baxley gave me a lopsided grin. "Are you saying I need to ask your father for your hand in marriage to make you an 'honest man' to preserve your modesty?"

I blushed at his comment. "No, but it's like, now what? We eat, then fuck?"

He did a shitty job of smothering his amusement. "Are you complaining or requesting I do a little romancing after I've wined and dined you this evening?"

"*No.*" I tried not to wince at how salty I sounded. "That would be way too weird."

"Why?"

It was such a deceptively simple question. I wasn't sure what specific objection I had, but the idea made me uncomfortable. All I could do was shrug and look away.

Baxley got up from the table and guided me to take a seat beside him on his couch in the living room. He looked at me with a softness I wasn't used to seeing, and it made me all fuzzy inside. "I meant it when I said nothing has to happen that you're not comfortable with. This isn't purely about the physical gratification of having sex."

"Sure, but it's at least a little bit about that." Sometimes I couldn't stop myself from being a smart-ass.

"I won't deny it, because what we did earlier was amazing." He took my hand in his, brushing his thumb over the back of mine. "But I'm not just after sex, shocking as that may be for you."

It was impossible not to grin. "When it's you, it *is* shocking."

He chuckled before turning serious. "I understand your concerns because I've never hidden how much I desire you. But I don't have a daily fuck quota that must be met in order for me to be satisfied."

I snorted in amusement. "A daily fuck quota? That's a new one."

"Please believe me when I say that if we spent the rest of tonight sitting here on my couch, shit-talking a terrible movie as we cuddled before going to bed, only to sleep, this is still the best damn day of my life. And I'm not saying that because of the mind-blowing sex. It has everything to do with the fact that you want to be with me."

I threw my arms around his neck and hugged him tight. When he drew me closer, it was utter perfection. "I'm sorry I'm being weird."

He soothingly rubbed me as I held him. "Are you overthinking the situation? Yes. But you're not being weird."

"What makes you say that?"

I didn't resist when he guided me to make eye contact while still allowing me to embrace him. "My suspicion is that you started worrying about once we finished dinner, your ass was mine. Am I wrong?"

His accuracy caused me to sit back with a pout. "You're not, but I wish you were."

Baxley made my heart tremble when he cupped my cheek in his hand. "Stop putting pressure on yourself. You've been attracted to women your whole life, which means your entire sexual drive has been dedicated to sticking your dick into them, right?"

"I mean, yeah, basically."

He stayed focused on explaining his logic to me. "Transitioning that need to be inside me was a much easier jump for you to make than being penetrated by me when you have *zero* experience."

"Um, I wouldn't say zero." I flushed scarlet as I

fessed up to something I had never told anyone before. "It's more like two."

Baxley's eyebrows both arched in surprise. "Oh, really? Do tell."

"The first time Julissa gave me a blow job, she stuck her fingers in my ass without my permission. It caught me so off guard, I came almost instantly. I got mad at her for it, but…"

His blue eyes lit up with excitement. "But your curiosity got the better of you, so you tried it on yourself while you jerked off?"

It shouldn't have surprised me he figured that out. "Yeah, but it felt bad, so I never did it again."

"You didn't use lube, did you?"

"Why would I? She only used her mouth to make her fingers wet, which is what I did."

He chuckled as he teased me. "Oh, you sweet summer child. You have so much to learn."

"It can't make *that* much of a difference."

"I have over a decade of experience that says otherwise," he said with a confidence that made me curious despite my reservations. "But we can save that for another time. Nothing has to happen tonight."

While I appreciated him giving me an out, it also brought out my competitive side. "Are you suggesting you could use only your fingers in my ass to get me off?"

"No, I'm guaranteeing it." His cocky confidence sent an unexpected thrill through me.

Before I could stop myself, the words "Then prove it" were out of my mouth. I could never resist a little friendly competition.

"Do you mean now or theoretically in the future?"

I got off the couch and tugged on his hand to pull him up to stand. "There's no time like the present, right?"

He followed me into the bedroom with a predatory gleam in his eyes that made my heart hammer. "I've gotta say, I'm a *big* fan of how fast you went from 'No way in hell' to 'Fuck me now' in a split second."

I took off my shirt and threw it aside. When he reached out to me, I stepped out of his reach. "Nope, no foreplay, either. I want you to prove you can make me come without doing anything else."

"You know I love a good challenge." He removed his clothes, allowing me to see he was already hard from the promise of being allowed to touch me. It was yet another sign of how sincere he was about his feelings toward me.

Once I stripped, I stretched out on his bed. For all my talk, my stomach fluttered with nervousness when he grabbed the bottle of lube and settled between my legs. "Only fingers," I reminded him, despite trusting him not to take advantage of me.

He circled my hole, making me shiver from the cool gel against my skin. "Are you sure? It would be better if you'd let me stimulate you in other ways at the same time."

"Yeah, but then I wouldn't know if I got off because of that or your fingers."

He snickered as he teased me with a hint of penetration. "Ah, so you're looking to maintain a control group in this *very* scientific experiment?"

"It's the only way I can make an informed decision." At least, it was what I told myself.

"Well, in that case." Baxley eased a single finger into me. Unlike when I had tried myself, it slid in easily and without pain. "Let's begin, shall we?"

It wasn't good or bad; it was just odd. "Is this supposed to be sexy? Because this is kind of like getting a prostate exam from my doctor."

"Let me remind you that *you're* the one insisting this be a clinical test." He snickered as he moved his finger inside me. "If you'd let me show how excellent I am at multitasking, it would be a lot sexier."

I scowled at his suggestion. "All it would prove is you're good at giving blow jobs, which would defeat the point of this experiment."

"There are plenty of other things I could do besides that." He brushed his lips against the inside of my thigh, allowing me to feel him speaking. "Even kissing you here could drive you wild."

It was too easy to poke fun at his ridiculous claim. "Ooh, baby, it's *soooo* sexy when you kiss me there. Fuck, that gets me *so* hot," I sarcastically teased him. I snorted and rolled my eyes for good measure. "Yeah, right."

The jerk had the audacity to make me eat my words when he sensuously kissed my thigh with a hint of suction, causing my breathing to hitch. He lavished it with oral attention as he trailed kisses up it. I was about to reprimand him when he nipped at my sensitive skin, making my dick twitch with need. It sent lust surging through me when combined with the way he stroked me inside.

To spare myself any further embarrassment, I flattened my leg onto the bed. "You can stop now, thanks."

"Why? Was it too *sexy* for you to handle?" His arrogant smirk stirred me up inside.

I lied like hell. "Nope."

As always, he called my bluff. "Funny, because *this* tells me a different story." He brushed the bead of precum from my tip that betrayed me.

I refused to give him the victory. "The only thing it proves is you're deliberately disobeying me."

"I'm not disobeying. I was merely providing an alternative suggestion in case you decided to change your mind."

Baxley stopped my retort when he added in a second finger. It made me shift under him at the strange sensation. "Not to disappoint you, but this really isn't doing it for me."

"Patience."

"Oh, you mean that thing I have none of? Sure,

okay." I scowled when he laughed again. "So, is this something you've always wanted to do to me?"

"Are you referring to being intimate with you or specifically having my fingers inside your ass?" He snickered, making me roll my eyes.

"I'd like to think your first thought when you saw me wasn't 'Damn, he's so hot, I need to finger-fuck his asshole.' But maybe that's just me."

His boisterous laughter filled me with warmth. "Something tells me you'll like my first thought even less."

"It's worse than that?"

He shook his head. "Only if you think 'I'm going to marry that man' is more unsettling than thoughts about how much I couldn't wait to get you in bed."

I propped myself up to get a better look at him. "Wait, your first thought was you wanted to *marry* me and not fuck me?"

"In my defense, marrying you would lead to a lifetime of sex with you, so it's not like I hadn't factored it into the equation." He flashed a lopsided grin at me. "I'm not sure if it makes it better or worse for you."

I dropped back onto the bed with a huff. "Even if I pondered it for hundreds of hours, I'd never reach a conclusion of how that could be *anyone's* first thought when they saw me, let alone *yours.*"

"Apparently, my inner caveman wanting to claim you as mine was feeling more romantic than usual."

"I still don't get it." Talk about a massive understatement. "You've always been a playboy. Why would you ever think of marriage before saying a single word to me?"

He shrugged. "You've got me. My initial reaction to you baffled me, so I don't have an answer for you."

It was strange thinking of him having that kind of romantic interest in me. "But now?"

"I have no doubts my gut instinct was right. You were meant to be mine."

A whimper escaped without my permission at his declaration when combined with him ghosting over something that made me weak in the knees.

"It sounds like *somebody* likes the idea of belonging to me."

He put more pressure on the spot, wrenching a moan from me at the unexpected burst of pleasure. It left me desperate to touch myself, but I resisted the urge.

"Should I mark you with a hickey to prove you're mine?" He curled his fingers, making me jerk from the explosion of ecstasy when combined with his sensual murmur. "Would you prefer me to scratch my nails down your back as you take me hard? Or should I come on you to claim you as mine?"

I squirmed as he pushed me closer to release. My body moved blindly as he fucked me with his fingers, making me ache for something I never expected to lust after. I had to bite my lower lip to hold in the pleas for more.

"Or should I tell you I love you over and over again until you love me, too?"

I cried out as I came without touching myself. Before I could catch my breath, Baxley put on a sensuous show by leaning forward to lick my stomach clean. It got me all spun up inside, especially when he moaned, "All mine," and sealed his promise with a kiss on the small mole above my hip.

Maybe later when I had a brain again, I'd be able to figure out why the hell that was so appealing.

Chapter Nine

WELL, well, well. What a delightfully unexpected turn of events it was to discover that the thought of being mine turned Callahan on, and the prospect of loving me made him come? It was the ultimate confidence boost to think that maybe his heart might belong to me someday after all.

He gestured for me to straddle over him. "Come here."

Curious about what he had in mind, I obeyed without smart-ass commentary for once.

He gave me a look-over before his gaze settled on my erection. It twitched from being the center of his attention. His voice was raw as he requested, "Show me."

"Show you what?"

There was no hesitation in his answer. "How I make you feel."

That sure sounded like an invitation to put on a performance, and I was more than happy to oblige. Taking myself in hand, I stroked my length. "You want to watch me get off while thinking about you?"

He silently nodded.

"Kinky." I grinned when he huffed at my description. "You disagree?"

"That hardly qualifies as a kink," he said in a miffed tone of voice.

"Sorry, baby, but watching me masturbate while I moan your name because you think it's hot falls squarely in the voyeuristic kink category."

He protested several times before he could form words. "*Baby?*"

"You told me to get off while thinking about you. In my mental movie theatre that plays featured films of us every night, that involves me calling you 'baby,' sorry."

He made a face at me. "Out of all possible nicknames, why did you choose '*baby*' for me?"

"Because when I touch myself and think about you, I always end up saying, 'Oh, baby, that feels so good!' It's a miracle I haven't slipped and called you that until now."

"I'd be fine if you never called me that, thanks."

I wasn't about to give up my nickname for him. His resistance meant I needed to step it up a notch. I arched my back and went into full porn star mode, moaning as sensuously as I could, "Oh, baby! Give me a little more. I'm so close! Baby, I—" Cutting myself off with a wordless cry, I jerked myself off as I grew more turned on by my theatrics.

Callahan's hand found purchase on my thighs as he caressed me with a teasing grin. "Fuck you very much for making 'baby' sound sexy."

"Would you rather me call you 'kumquat' instead?" I snickered at the idea. It sounded obscene, even though it wasn't.

"Don't call me that in front of the guys, and we'll be fine."

I grinned at him. "You're only 'baby' behind bedroom doors. Got it." I couldn't wait to tease him by calling him "babe" on a technicality the next time we hung out with Alessandro and Lachlan. His blushing embarrassment would *so* be worth it.

Callahan's possessive grip as his hands crept higher to my hips sent me soaring.

It looked like it was time to step things up a notch. "I'm imagining you starting off soft and slow as you show me how much you love me. But then we unleash our passion, and you can't stop yourself from fucking me hard and fast. It's so hot thinking about you coming inside me, baby. *So damn hot.*"

"You want me to rail you to prove I love you? Interesting." He continued observing me before he tilted his head in consideration. "What do I call you in your dreams?"

"You usually call me 'sweetheart,' especially when

151

I'm sucking your dick." My hand picked up speed as I remembered how good it felt when he did that in my fantasies. "It started as a joke, but we both secretly like it."

"Somehow, it doesn't seem very romantic to say, 'I can't wait to see you blow your load on me, sweetheart,'" he said with a snicker. "Wow, I never would have pegged you for a 'baby' and 'sweetheart' guy. You're just full of surprises today."

I grinned because he wasn't wrong. "You still have a lot to learn about me."

"I'm pretty sure I can master calling you 'sweetheart' if that's what it takes to get you to come." He surprised me by reaching back to grope my ass hard before giving me a spank.

The unexpected and welcomed sting shoved me over the edge. My cum spurted all over his stomach as I cried out, "Baby!"

His eyebrows arched upward. "So, was it the 'sweetheart' or the spanking that did that?"

"Little bit of column A, little bit of column B." It felt better than I had expected to hear him say, "Sweetheart," for real.

He looked up at me with curiosity. "But spanking? Really? *You*?"

"Why is that weird?"

"Because you seem like the guy who gets off on doing the spanking, not being the one getting spanked."

"As long as it involves you, I'm good with almost anything."

He grinned at that. "*Almost* anything? Where do you draw the line?"

"I'd try anything for you." I moved off him to grab a tissue to clean him off. Stretching out beside him, I snuggled closer.

His mischievous grin was too cute for words. "That almost makes me want to develop a *really* weird kink, just to see if I could get you into it."

"Be careful what you wish for. It's all funny when it starts as a joke, but then you might get into it for real," I teased him.

He reached over and guided me closer for a sweet kiss that melted me. His smile after we parted was beautiful. "Well, you've convinced me I can handle what comes next, so here's hoping."

His words overjoyed me, but I wanted to pace myself. "We'll save that fun for tomorrow. For now, I just want to cuddle with my baby for the rest of the night."

He repeated, "Baby," before breaking into a fit of giggles. "It'll take a while to get used to that."

"That's fine. We've got all the time in the world, and I'm grateful for every second I spend with you."

"Your romantic side is a lot to process, but I must admit, I'm kinda loving you're secretly schmoopy. How have you hidden it from me for so long?"

"Because I'm surprisingly masochistic for a sadist."

We both laughed at that as we continued lazing together until sleep claimed us both for the night.

Chapter Ten

CALLAHAN

I WOKE up ready to fuck. Yesterday had proven that Baxley wasn't all talk, so I was in the mood for more experimentation. Thankfully, I wasn't the only one with morning wood that wished to kick off the day in a sexy way.

Since he was spooning me from behind, his erection pressed against my ass. It sent a nervous thrill through me as I rocked against it. "*Bax.*"

Hearing his name earned me a sleepy rumble, but he still didn't wake up. Determined to have my way, I guided his hand to my rigid length. "It's time to get up, sweetheart."

His grip around my dick tightened as he stroked me. "You're already up."

"So are you. Let's do this."

He kissed along the curve of my shoulder, sending

shivers down my spine. "Do what? Appreciate every inch of you until you come?"

"That sounds good later. Right now, I'm dying of curiosity and from the need to get off. You can fix both problems for me."

His sleepy chuckle sent a shudder through me. Since when was that hot? "Now I'm the one that's curious. What are you hoping for?"

I moved his hand away so I could roll over to face him. It came as a genuine surprise to see him looking at me with open adoration and amusement. I opted for a blunt approach. "Take me."

His lips quirked up into a smirk. "Home?"

I reached out and tweaked his nipple, making him hiss in pain. "No, jackass. Wow, you're *really* slow on the uptake first thing in the morning."

He rubbed his sore chest, but he looked far from displeased. "That was an attempt at humor."

"Ohhhh, it was so funny, I forgot to laugh," I said, my voice dripping with sarcasm.

It earned me a snicker before he leaned forward and kissed me. Having expected a hard and punishing kiss, I was unprepared for how tender it was. It stirred a desire within me that had nothing to do with how horny and desperate I was to get off.

"And how would you like me to take you?"

I huffed in annoyance that he was making me spell it out for him. "In the ass."

His blue eyes were bright with amusement. "I

figured that much. What I meant was do you want me to make gentle love to you, or are you down to fuck?"

"As long as your dick is inside me and I'm having a good time, that's all that matters to me right now, sweetheart."

His next kiss was more demanding as he claimed my mouth with passionate need. Damn, I had *really* underestimated how much he enjoyed being called "sweetheart." It baffled me that someone like him wanted to be addressed by that nickname, but I didn't have the brain cells left to dedicate to thinking too deeply on the matter. Instead, I laced my fingers through his hair and pulled him closer as I drowned in him.

He didn't give me a moment to breathe as he began working my body up into a frenzy with nipping kisses and teasing touches. It was so good that I was in danger of coming before we reached the sex part. Everything became white noise in my head as he went down on me while he stretched me with his fingers. The combined pleasure was far more intense than I had expected. Seeing him sucking my dick as if it would reward him with the manna of the gods was such a huge turn-on.

I tried to warn him I was close, but my mouth could only make erotic whimpers and gasps as I pleaded for release. My grip on his hair tensed as every muscle in my body grew taut in anticipation of my orgasm building up inside me. When he deep-throated me while curling his fingers with the right amount of pressure, my back arched as I came, crying out his name. I collapsed on the bed as he licked me clean and withdrew, leaving me feeling empty.

Baxley short-circuited my brain when he sat on his haunches and put on a show of stroking his arousal. "Can you handle more, baby?"

Competitive to a fault, I reached between my legs and ran my fingers over my hole. "Give me all you've got, sweetheart."

"Fuck, that's *so goddamn sexy*," he breathed in a rush as he repositioned himself. The head of his cock pressed against my entrance, making me tense with nerves. "Remember to breathe and relax. It'll be weird at first, but I promise it gets better."

"That sure sounds like, 'This is going to hurt, but suck it up,' to me."

"You'll be fine. Promise." He pushed into me, causing me to inhale sharply as I waited for the pain to begin. Instead, it was an awkward stretching sensation that I couldn't imagine would ever turn into something pleasureful.

It took forever for him to get inside me. "While I appreciate you taking it slow so it doesn't hurt, this is verging closer to boring than it is to sexy."

"How is it my fault that you have a short attention span and no patience?" He snorted in amusement. "Trust me, your ass will thank you later for allowing me to be considerate and not drilling you straight into the mattress your first time."

I hooked my legs around his waist to force him deeper, without success. "Can't we find a happy medium somewhere in between a glacial pace and ripping me a new one? This is *agonizingly* slow."

"Fuss all you want, but I'm not rushing you. The last thing I wish to do is hurt you and then have you ban me from ever doing this again."

"Come on, sweetheart. Fuck me," I whined as I made another attempt at making him speed up.

Baxley finally bottomed out, his body flush against mine. "We'll get to that, I promise."

I tensed around him, resulting in his fingers digging into my hips. "This may be new to me, but I'm pretty sure you're supposed to be moving."

"Oh, *you're* giving *me* lessons on how to do this?" He leaned forward, drawing a gasp from me at the shift in angles. "This should be fun."

"It would be if you moved!" When he started with slow movements, I groaned as I squirmed under him. "Is there some reason you're insisting on torturing me? Icebergs fuck faster than this."

I regretted my comment when he laughed so hard that he stopped moving. "And how, pray tell, does an iceberg fuck?"

"With their dickicles and faster than this, I can guaran-damn-tee you that."

He only laughed harder. "*Dickicles?*"

"Yeah, icebergs *obviously* would have dick icicles. So, dickicles."

Baxley hit the point of extreme amusement where no sound came out. It made me crack up and almost forget that we were in the middle of trying to have sex. He gasped through his laughter, "Wait, does that make ice floes the iceberg's cum?"

I snickered so hard that I snorted, setting him off again as his body shook with amusement. The sheer absurdity of the conversation made me lose it, making me wipe away tears of mirth from my eyes. "I'm going to say yes because that's *hilarious*. Now, are we doing this, or should we keep laughing?"

"I'm pretty sure we can do both." Baxley proved it by still chuckling as he moved again.

I stretched out as I got used to him inside me. It didn't hurt, which was good, but it also felt like pressure without a point.

"Wow, I can literally hear you thinking, 'So, this is anal sex? Meh.'" Baxley sounded more amused than annoyed by it, thankfully.

"No offense, but this isn't much of anything." I shrugged as I tried to make myself comfortable. "Your fingers promised me a lot more than what I'm getting. So, either they're more talented than your dick, or I'm not that into anal."

Instead of being offended, Baxley guided my legs from around his waist to drape over his shoulders as he shifted positions to lean forward. Although I felt weirdly exposed at that angle, my heart skipped a beat from the way he gripped my thighs. "You're always so impatient."

"And yet, you're still taking your sweet-ass time, anyway." I scowled at him, since he knew better than anyone that I was all about instant gratification.

"Get ready, baby, because I'm about to blow your mind."

I was about to taunt him about being all talk, but he picked up speed as he thrust into me with more force. The new position let him hit deeper than before, making my body tense from the unexpected bursts of desire it sent racing up my spine. "*Oh!*"

The smug bastard gloated as he took me harder, which somehow made him sexier. He wrung a whimper out of me when his hands slid down my thighs to grope my ass. My body rocked into the sensation as my erection returned.

When I thought I had a handle on the sensations, Baxley switched things up on me. The mixture of short and fast pumps of his hips alternating between long and hard thrusts made me cry out as I arched under him. It was better than what his fingers and mouth had offered me. The longer it went on, the more I lost my mind as he sent me soaring on an unbelievable high.

"That's it, baby," he all but purred. "Let me hear that gorgeous voice of yours calling out to me."

It was a complete mystery to me how he had

rewired my brain so quickly, making me respond to being called by that nickname. "Bax, Baxley, sweetheart, *please!*" I applauded myself for still having the wherewithal to cover all my bases during mind-blowing sex.

He rewarded me by almost bending me in half and taking me hard and fast. To my shock, I fucking *loved* it. I shouted in ecstasy as I arched up from the overwhelming sensations bombarding me. It unlocked something deep within me, turning me into a wanton creature. "More!"

He obeyed without question or smart-ass commentary, which was its own turn-on. His nails digging into my thighs made me bite my lip to stop from shouting at how good everything was. He played my body expertly as I writhed under him, mindless with lust and desperate for more.

I caressed myself to heighten my enjoyment while moaning, "Fuck, this feels so good, sweetheart!"

His reaction caught me off guard. He pushed all the way in and came inside me as he called out, "Baby!" Knowing I could make my best friend climax by calling him a cutesy nickname was a powerful piece of knowledge that I looked forward to exploiting later.

Baxley reached down to stroke my hard-on, sending fiery bursts of ecstasy flaring through me. All it took was a few strokes to trigger my release, a shout getting caught in my throat as I came a second time.

I was too overwhelmed by the detonation of sexual satisfaction to process anything other than how *incredible* I felt. As a result, I didn't resist when he pulled out and guided my legs off his shoulders to the bed. Instead, I tugged him up for a hungry kiss. I prayed like hell it told him how much I *loved* the experience, even if the foreplay part had been unbearably long for my tastes.

When we parted, he lay beside me, then reached over to caress my cheek. "Do you care to revise your opinion about my dick's abilities now?"

It was *such* a Baxley thing to ask. I couldn't stop myself from bursting into laughter. The normalcy of it all was reassuring that he was still my best friend, even though I was now his baby, too. "Next time, a little less foreplay and a lot more fucking would be great."

"Well, if you're offering me another chance, then I think I've proven my point," he said with smug satisfaction. I'd let him have it since he had rocked my world.

I gestured at the mess we had made. "Clearly. My stomach looks like it's covered in arctic ice floes, thanks to you."

As I had hoped, he cracked up again as he gasped, "*Dickicles!*" He kept laughing, making me lose it right along with him. It meant everything to me that he thought my immature sense of humor was funny, instead of rolling his eyes and telling me to grow up like my ex-girlfriends had. That felt almost as good as what we had just done.

When we quieted down, I reached over and tugged him down for a tender kiss. I knew how rare it was to see the gentle side of Baxley, which made me treasure it even more. Dating my best friend was *so* awesome.

Epilogue

BAXLEY

THE CLOSER WE got to Lachlan's place, the more uptight Callahan became. He sighed in agitation as he ran his fingers through his auburn hair. "You know they're going to be dicks about this, right?"

"In their defense, we busted their balls about them hooking up, too. Turnabout is fair play." I glanced over at him. "What are you worried about? Our group dynamic has always involved joking about stuff."

He shrugged with a scowl. "I don't know. I'm being weird."

Hoping to console him, I reached over and caressed the nape of his neck. "It'll be fine, baby. If their disappointment over us not getting together the other day is any indication, they'll be happy. Plus, we can go on double dates now."

He seemed skeptical. "How's that different than all four of us hanging out like normal?"

"We get to make out while we do it." Since I was at a stoplight, I leaned over and gave him a teasing kiss.

He pushed me back with a huff. "I forbid you from giving me an erection around them."

"Good luck with that." I snorted in amusement at his big talk. "If you can swim with me in the pool without getting one, you're a better man than me."

"At least I had the decency to politely ignore that when it happened before," he muttered as he crossed his arms over his chest. "Now, it'll be my problem."

"Oh, poor baby. What a terrible hardship you have to endure over the fact that your boyfriend finds you arousing." I laughed as he made a face at me. "What are you so worried about? Do you think the same thing won't happen to Lachlan and Alessandro? Hell, I'm hoping it does, because it gives us time to enjoy ourselves while they go off to do the same in the shower."

"We are *not* having sex in Lachlan's house."

I chuckled at his naivety. "Sure, you say that now. But I'll remind you of this conversation when you're dying to come later."

"That *won't* happen."

I said nothing as I let him cling to his illusions for the time being.

"Besides, we already had our fun this morning,"

he reminded me with a blush. That was an under-statement, considering the sexual turn my attempt at helping him put on sunscreen had taken at my place before we left.

When we got out of the car after I parked in Lachlan's driveway, I pulled Callahan into my embrace. "Relax, baby. They'll tease us, we'll make fun of them, and then continue with our day. You have nothing to worry about. Other than getting an inconvenient hard-on, of course."

He rolled his eyes at me, but he still hugged me back. "Remember, if you call me 'baby' in front of them today, I'm not going home with you tonight. Got it?"

Even though I didn't believe he had the willpower to resist me, I gave him a sweet kiss. "Promise."

Our friends were lounging together in the pool on the rainbow unicorn float, with Alessandro in Lach-lan's lap. I couldn't resist joking with them about it. "The poor flamingo is going to get jealous now that you two are shacking it up with only the unicorn."

"We left it for you and Callahan," Alessandro said.

Before I could get in a retort, Lachlan beat me to it. "I'm amazed you're here. I figured you wouldn't let Callahan leave your bed long enough to come hang out today."

"Oh, I'm confident they've had fun in more places than just Baxley's bedroom," Alessandro added with a wicked grin. "Based on Callahan blushing so hard that he already looks sunburnt, I'm assuming we're right."

Rather than answering, I took off my shirt and kicked off my sandals to cannonball splash them. Sure, it was immature, but those were the rules of horseplaying in a pool. Callahan followed suit, although he was careful to keep his distance from me. Him being so cautious to avoid my temptation amused the hell out of me and endeared him to me even more.

Since the flamingo float was free, I hopped onto it and made myself comfortable. "Are you asking for a demonstration? Because I'm pretty sure my boyfriend is going to decline the opportunity to indulge your voyeurism kink."

Alessandro lit up with genuine delight. "You went for the full boyfriend experience and not just a little experimentation? Good for you, Callahan. See? I told you leaving the flamingo float open for them was a good idea."

"You know me. I never half-ass anything," he said with a grin, although his cheeks were still flushed.

"Yes, luckily for me, he whole-asses everything," I added with a smirk that earned laughs from our friends.

Lachlan looked equally happy. "Then congratulations are in order."

"We couldn't have done it without you taking the plunge first, so I owe you, Lachlan," I told him. "And

Alessandro for being so tempting that you couldn't say no anymore."

Lachlan grinned as he addressed Callahan. "So, how much do you regret waiting to give in to Baxley's advances?"

To my delight, Callahan made himself comfortable on my lap without overturning the flamingo float. "I'm having way more fun making up for lost time than wasting my energy on regrets."

His answer was too precious not to react. I hugged him tightly and pressed a kiss to his temple. "Aww, you say the sweetest things, babe."

He squeaked in protest. "You promised you wouldn't call me that!" Our friends got a good laugh out of that.

"No, I promised to only call you 'baby' behind closed doors," I reminded him. "You never took 'babe' off the table, so it's fair game."

"Fine, *sweetie*, if that's how you want to play it." His quick-witted nature to shorten "sweetheart" in such a way to get payback made me love him even more.

Alessandro cracked up as Callahan fumed in embarrassment. "Oh, that's *adorable*. Looks like we need to up our boyfriend game, Lachlan. They've got us beat on cute nicknames."

"So, am I supposed to call you 'snookums' now?" Lachlan's droll delivery made his line even funnier to me.

"If not, there's always 'cuddle muffin' as an alternative," I joked.

Callahan laughed. "And to think, I could have been 'cuddle muffin' instead of your baby."

"I'd rather stick with 'snookums,' thanks," Alessandro said with another laugh. "We'll work on it later."

It was too tempting to rib them a little. "Preferably naked and behind closed doors, am I right?"

"Despite your assertions to the contrary, I don't have a voyeurism kink, so yes, the door will be shut to stop you from getting your perv on."

I laughed at his answer. "That's fine with me, because it means Callahan and I can enjoy ourselves, too."

Callahan huffed. "We are *not* doing that!"

"You'd rather have them watch us? How kinky, babe. I'm into it."

He made a noise of protest before elbowing me in payback, making me laugh.

"It's nice to know some things never change," Lachlan said, watching our antics with amusement.

I nuzzled Callahan. "If I quit teasing you, you'd think I didn't love you anymore."

"You just like doing it to make me blush," he complained.

"Now you're catching on." When he protested, I tilted his chin toward me to capture his lips in a heated kiss. It earned catcalls from our friends, but none of that mattered when I had my best friend and the greatest love of my life in my arms, kissing me like nobody was watching.

Best summer ever.

Want to see more of the guys? **Download bonus scenes from both books today**!

In the mood for more sexiness between best friends involving a bi awakening for both guys? **Read Bet on Love next to enjoy Rhys and Lucien's sizzling romance**.

Thank You

Thank you for reading **Suntastic Fun**. Reviews are crucial for helping other readers discover new books to enjoy. If you want to share your love for Lachlan, Alessandro, Baxley, and Callahan, please leave a review. I'd really appreciate it!

Recommending my work to others is also a huge help. Don't hesitate to give this book a shout-out in your favorite book rec group to spread the word.

Bet on Love

AVAILABLE NOW

After Rhys wakes up married to his best man, he never expects to fall in love with his new husband. Will their surprise romance survive the wedding bells?

If you love friends to lovers, dual bi awakening, second chance, gay romances that are sweet and steamy, **read Bet on Love today by using the QR code below**!

Acknowledgments

I hope you enjoyed Lachlan, Alessandro, Baxley, and Callahan's romances! They're such a fun group of friends and the perfect way to celebrate summer fun.

A special thank you goes out to my amazing team of beta readers of Amy Mitchell, Raquel Riley, Lindsay Porter, Tammy Jones, Lisa Klein, Kylie Anderson, Cilla May, Dylan Pope, Jennifer Sharon, Missy Kretschmer, and Ashley Krystalf! I'm so lucky to be friends with such amazing people.

I'm incredibly grateful to Shelia Kilgore, Beth Barton, Tammy Jones, Gabriela, and my other Ko-fi supporters who help make it possible for me to be a full-time author.

I also want to thank everyone who recommends my books in Facebook rec threads. It means the world to me that you share my books with other readers. I'm also filled with endless gratitude to all of my ARC readers for their kind and helpful reviews.

I'm blessed to work with Pam, Sandra, and Cate. I'm so grateful that they always help me shine my brightest.

Also, I'd like to thank Kira Jackson and my other

readers who have sent me such kind emails asking when they could get a paperback of this series. That feedback was so helpful, so thank you for reaching out to me!

I can't wait to meet again in **Bet on Love**!

About the Author

WWW.ARIELLAZOELLE.COM

Ariella Zoelle adores steamy, funny, swoony romances where couples are allowed to just be happy. She writes low angst stories full of heat, humor, and heart. But sometimes she's in the mood for something with a bit more angst and drama. If you are too, check out her A.F. Zoelle books.

Get a bonus chapter by using the QR code below!

Made in the USA
Columbia, SC
25 September 2023

23310212R00102